Things Cannoli Get Better

Baker's Rise Mysteries

Book Nine

R. A. Hutchins

Copyright © 2023 Rachel Anne Hutchins

All rights reserved.

The characters, locations and events portrayed in this story are wholly the product of the author's imagination. Any similarity to any persons, whether living or dead, is purely coincidental.

Cover Design by Molly Burton at cozycoverdesigns.com

ISBN: 9798393620813

For everyone who dances like no one is watching,

Hilda and Reggie salute you!

CONTENTS

*If you follow this list in order, you will have made some perfect **Lemon Ricotta Cannoli** to enjoy whilst you read!*

1)	Put on your favourite apron	1
2)	Ingredients for the Cannoli shell:	5
3)	30g butter	12
4)	2 tablespoons brown sugar	20
5)	1 tablespoon golden syrup	27
6)	2 tablespoons plain flour	36
7)	1/2 teaspoon almond essence	43
8)	Icing sugar, to serve	51
9)	Ingredients for the lemon and ricotta filling:	60
10)	500g fresh ricotta	67
11)	75g icing sugar, sifted	75
12)	1 tablespoon lemon juice	83
13)	1 tablespoon lemon zest	90
14)	Preheat oven to 180°C. Line 2 oven trays with baking paper	97
15)	Combine butter, brown sugar and golden syrup in a pan	104
16)	Stir over medium heat for 2-3 minutes, until sugar dissolves	112
17)	Remove from heat and quickly stir in flour and almond essence	118
18)	Cool for 5 minutes	126
19)	Place well-spaced tablespoons of mixture onto trays	135
20)	Bake for 7 minutes or until bubbling, and spread to 10cm in diameter	143
21)	Remove from oven and let cool for 1 min	151

22) Working quickly, lift each one and wrap loosely around the handle of a large rolling pin	159
23) Then leave to set for 1 minute before gently slipping off and transferring to a wire rack to cool	166
24) Repeat with remaining mixture	172
25) To make filling, combine ricotta, icing sugar, lemon juice and zest	178
26) Mix well and keep chilled until required	184
27) Spoon mixture into cooled shells and serve dusted with icing sugar	191
28) Put your feet up and enjoy your sweet treat with a cup of tea and a great book!	196
Excerpt from "Fresh as a Daisy" – Lillymouth Mysteries Book One	205
Baker's Rise Mysteries Book Ten	213
The Lillymouth Mysteries Books 1 & 2	215
About The Author	219
Other books by this Author	221

ONE

"I still don't understand why we need to have foreign food."

"Plenty of people in this country enjoy Italian food now, Betty," Flora bit down on the need to shout the words across the large kitchen at The Rise and instead forced a smile as she repeated the same thing for the third time that morning, "there's even that new Italian restaurant over in Witherham who are catering the pizzas and pasta for us."

"Aye well, I could have made us some lovely mini Victoria sponges instead of having to learn a new recipe at my age," Betty harumphed as she kneaded the ingredients to a smooth dough in much the same way as she would with any similar mixture, "I mean, who will even like these little cannons?"

"Cannoli," Tanya corrected once again, the exasperation clear in her voice.

"Whatever they are, they sound fiddly, and don't even get me started on the fact we have to fry them tomorrow! Even a halfwit knows you don't fry good bakes."

"Well, some people do bake them in the oven, but we've been recommended a recipe that uses a frying pan, so you can skip that part if you like," Flora said, secretly praying that her friend would do just that, "if you need to get your hair set for the big event or anything…"

The village had been preparing for the fancy dress, Italian themed, murder mystery evening for a few weeks now, and excitement levels had reached a peak rarely seen in Baker's Rise. Costumes had been made or ordered, a troupe of actors were coming to perform the scenes which would enable the audience to try to guess the murderer, and a large buffet of Italian food was on the menu.

"I've opened the windows in the function room," Genie Blanchette said as she entered the kitchen, "it's stuffy in there now the temperature's heated up." It was indeed very balmy weather for June in the northeast of England, as evidenced by the dripping wet little parrot who was enjoying splashing about in a makeshift bath in the sink.

"Ciao bella!" He squawked happily, the housekeeper having become one of his favourite people since she started work at the big house last autumn. Unfortunately, Reggie had also spent the past day overseeing rehearsals around the house, and had picked up a few phrases from the cast members. Combined with watching 'The Godfather' with Harry, Flora knew his repertoire on the evening of the event would be eclectic at best.

At first, Flora had been somewhat resentful at having to host the charity occasion at all, it having come about because she had promised the Blanchette sisters they could hold an Italian evening at The Rise. As time had gone on, however, and she had seen how the whole village had pitched in, Flora had decided that they all deserved this evening of spritz and sleuthing. Things had been thankfully quiet in Baker's Rise since the murder at last year's Autumn Fayre, and life had settled into a cosy routine which Flora was keen to perpetuate. Besides which, they had much to celebrate. The vicar's wife, Sally, had come through her treatment for a brain tumour and was well on the way to full health. Even though they wouldn't be there for the event as they were taking a much-needed family holiday on the south coast, Flora knew that both Sally and James were thrilled the proceeds from the ticket sales were going to Cancer Research UK. Her groundsman, Laurie, and his wife Rosa had undergone an unsuccessful round of IVF in the springtime, but had just announced last month that they were pregnant with a little miracle, conceived naturally, and baby fever had struck the village ladies once again, further fuelled by the fact that Flora and Adam had themselves been recently approved as foster parents and were expecting their first child any time now.

Yes, Flora thought as she mixed and kneaded, *so much cause for celebration.*

TWO

Flora woke up the next morning with a To Do list longer than her arm.

"We'd better get going if we're going to get this lot done before Tanya's shift at the tearoom finishes," Flora said, "she needs the afternoon off to get her hair done."

"Ah, I've got to wait in for this delivery love. We can't afford to have it sent back to the post office," Adam replied, not even trying to hide the look of relief in his eyes. A trip around the village, stopping at Lily's farm shop, Jean's convenience store, Rosa's embroidery studio and the pub wasn't his idea of an ideal morning. Not because of the exercise involved, or the shopping even, but more because he knew his wife and the villagers well enough to know that at least ten minutes of chatting would occur at each venue.

"Well if you hadn't left our costumes till the last minute…" Flora snapped back, slipping her feet into a well-worn pair of flat slingbacks and hunting around for her keys. After her choice of outfit for them both for the fayre last autumn, her husband had insisted on being in charge of their ensemble this time around. Much to Flora's annoyance, he had left the task until the last minute, steadfastly refusing to let his wife know which characters they would be portraying at the party. Flora had never been good with being kept in the dark and had been hoping to have a sneak peek at the outfits when they arrived and then to just send them back if necessary. As it was, with the murder mystery event due to take place the following evening, Flora knew that whatever the parcel contained was what she would have to wear.

Would Adam want to get a tiny bit of revenge for the Captain Hook garb she'd forced him to wear? Only time would tell, and Flora didn't have any to spare thinking about it now.

"My Flora," Reggie squawked hopefully, coming to land on her shoulder at the familiar signs that she was about to leave the coach house.

"Not this time, Reggie, you stay with Adam," Flora was still rushing around.

"Per favore, pleasy cheesy," the little parrot said, in his most obsequious tone, rubbing his downy soft head feathers against Flora's neck.

"Still a no," Flora replied, earning her a shriek of "You old trout!" as her feisty friend launched himself off her shoulder and onto the kitchen bench, no doubt expecting his affrontery to be massaged away with a bit of fruity bribery.

"You get going, I'll get him some blueberries," Adam said, well used to the routine by now.

The early summer air was warm with barely a breeze and Flora could tell as soon as she stepped outside that it was going to be another glorious day. Her first stop was the vicarage to speak to Christopher Cartwright. The man had agreed to stay on as co-vicar once James had returned to the role after Sally's illness, given that the parish also covered the churches in Witherham and Lower Snugly. The trust which Flora had set up to contribute funding to the church and its upkeep could afford the two salaries, since James had chosen to reduce his hours and therefore his responsibilities on his return. Until the springtime, Reverend Cartwright had lived happily up at the manor house, but as his relationship with Genie Blanchette was progressing quickly, he had deemed it inappropriate for them both to continue living under one – albeit extremely large – roof. Flora knew that Genie was hoping wedding bells might be heard from the church tower very soon, and that Christopher's lodging at the vicarage would only be temporary.

Unbeknownst to her housekeeper, the new vicar had taken Flora into his confidence, and expressed a desire to pose a very specific question to Genie on the night of the big Italian-themed event, and it was the exact logistics of this which Flora was going to discuss with the man now.

The vicarage seemed eerily quiet and empty without the familiar squeals of the Marshall girls as Flora waited in the sitting room while the vicar made them a cup of tea. Ordinarily, she would have joined the man in the kitchen so they could chat whilst he filled the kettle and prepared the teapot, as they had so many times up at The Rise. However, Cartwright seemed distracted and ill at ease today, so Flora was giving him some space. Unsure whether it was the nerves setting in in advance of the life changing decision he hoped Genie would make the next day, or something else entirely, Flora had never seen the man quite so out of fettle.

"Here we go, Flora, black coffee, no sugar," he said as he sat the tray down on the mahogany coffee table between them and took the seat opposite her.

Flora, a lifelong tea drinker by preference, had never in her life asked for coffee without either cream or milk, and if she had she would certainly have needed some sugar to make it palatable. Nevertheless, not wanting to appear rude, Flora voiced her thanks and silently decided the man must be in a much worse place than he had first appeared.

They dispensed with the pleasantries – the usual comments on the weather, the size of the weekly congregation and the wellbeing of several elderly residents – before Flora could bite her tongue no longer.

"Christopher, is everything okay? I mean, you seem… a little out of sorts if you don't mind me saying."

The man ran his fingers through his neatly shorn hair, adjusted his dog collar, picked up his own teacup and set it down again without drinking so much as a sip before finally replying, "Actually, Flora, I received some rather unwelcome mail today and it has me all in a tiz-woz."

"Oh?" Flora asked, not wanting to sound too nosy but also very keen to hear more. You couldn't live in Baker's Rise for long without succumbing to the general feeling that everything was everybody's news. The archetypal goldfish bowl. Of course, Flora would never consider herself a gossip…

"Yes, quite disturbing actually."

"Really?"

"Extremely worrying, in fact."

Oh for goodness sake just tell me, Flora smiled and nodded encouragingly. The silence stretched between them until at length she felt forced to speak again, "Perhaps you could show me? If it's not too personal, that is?"

"Ah, yes, well, yes…" He produced a white envelope from his pocket, rather crumpled as if either he or the sender had already fingered it many times.

Flora took the offered missive and immediately scanned the front of the envelope for any clues as to its origin. There was no postmark, no stamp in fact, which indicated that the letter had been hand delivered. The inky inscription, which was smudged and appeared to have been written in considerable hurry, read simply 'The Vicar' which for some reason annoyed Flora immediately. Perhaps because the ambiguity as to the intended recipient meant it could equally have been meant for James Marshall.

Pushing this aside, Flora removed the single sheaf of paper from within. It appeared to have been torn out of a lined notebook or journal, there being a wide margin at the top of the page with a prompt for the date, as well as an uneven, ripped side on the left. Flora was beginning to get the sinking feeling in her stomach that told her something wasn't quite right. It was all rather reminiscent of the threatening letters she had received that time Reggie was birdnapped by their erstwhile postman. Memories Flora wasn't keen to relive.

Forcing her attention back to the letter in hand, a rather childlike scrawl was made further illegible by the smudged ink from what appeared to be an old fashioned fountain pen – the blots and drops familiar from Flora's childhood when her father enjoyed collecting such writing tools. The majority of the space on the page had been left blank, save for the one sentence roughly scribbled in the centre:

Leave now before you regret staying in Baker's Rise.

THREE

"I'm not sure what to say," Flora handed the letter and envelope back to Reverend Cartwright so quickly and suddenly, it were as if the paper itself were on fire.

The man himself appeared to share her distaste for the worrisome communication, as he shoved the notepaper back inside the sleeve so hurriedly that the whole thing became further crumpled, before he gave up half way and threw it haphazardly onto the coffee table where it lay as if taunting them to question its contents.

"I guess it could be for James Marshall?" Flora added, trying to grasp onto any positive angle.

"Considering everyone in the three villages knows the family are away this month, and since James is loved by all, I think that's highly unlikely… but thank you for trying to cheer me up, Flora, I appreciate the sentiment."

"Okay, well, I think it's best if we take this round to Adam. He's got a lot of experience with… this kind of thing," Flora nodded resolutely, glad to pass off any responsibility she may have felt for looking into the message.

"Good thinking. Would you like to take it back with you?" Christopher caught Flora's grimace and thought better of the suggestion, "Actually, I'll walk round there now."

"Perfect, he'll definitely be at home in the coach house. He's expecting our Italian fancy dress. I'm hoping for something glamorous but classy, you know, kind of Sophia Loren meets Cleopatra," Flora enthused, sighing wistfully. Of course, the vicar wasn't the slightest bit interested in her nervous blathering, so Flora quickly added, "I'll finish my round of visits then I'll meet you back there as we haven't even had a chance to discuss how you're going to pop the question!"

Flora stood and gathered her things, the offensive hot beverage remaining untouched on the table.

Flora took longer than she'd intended, discussing Italian flags with Rosa, garlic bread with Lily and getting her own shopping at Jean's. Then she'd taken the weight off her feet at The Bun in the Oven with a cheeky glass of red and a chat with Shona about the wines for the mystery evening before hurrying back home just before lunchtime.

"Not that jerk! Stupid git!" Flora heard as she walked up the gravel path to their cottage. Indeed, upon entering she found her husband in almost as foul a mood as her little parrot.

Adam whisked her into the kitchen and whispered, "Where've you been? Reggie took an immediate dislike to the reverend being here. He's been shrieking like this for the past hour and a half – we can barely hear ourselves think! It's embarrassing, Flora, especially when we're discussing a potential threat. Not that there was much evidence to consider, I've been making awkward chitchat for the past hour and you know how that's not my strong suit…"

"Reggie normally likes Cartwright when he's up at the big house," Flora whispered back, filling the kettle and plating up some of the Viennese whirls she'd treated them to from Lily's.

"Aye well, he seemingly can't stand the bloke now,"

Adam made a quick return to the sitting room as Flora gave her parrot the biggest grape she could find. More to keep him quiet than anything.

"My Flora. So cosy," he cooed.

"Hmm, someone isn't in Adam's good books," Flora replied, tapping him on the beak but unable to feel cross with the little fella.

"So you think it'll be okay?" James asked again, helping himself to his third cake and seemingly oblivious to his hostess's scrutiny as he sought Adam's reassurance.

"Well, as I've said we've not got a lot to go on. Between you and Flora here, any fingerprints will likely have been smudged, but it's worth a shot so leave it with me and I'll drop it into the station when I get a moment. It may be later in the week, mind, after the big event," Adam added, his gaze resting on Flora who was rather unsubtly staring at the clock, "Or actually, McArthur and Timpson are coming tomorrow night – off the clock – but I could pass it to them then."

"Well, if that's settled, we'd better be getting across to the tearoom," Flora chimed in, before remembering that she hadn't actually spoken to the vicar about the following evening, "Oh! And what about tomorrow?

Do we need to set anything up, props, flowers or suchlike? Do you want a crowd or a private moment?" Flora asked, rummaging in her bag for her phone and opening the notes app which was her lifeline for all things event related.

"I, ah, well, I think a quiet moment out in the gardens will be fine, perhaps the rose garden? Though I know there won't be many in bloom. Then, if, ah, the answer is in the affirmative, so to speak, Genie and I can announce it at the end of the evening. Would that be okay?"

"Absolutely, you just give me the cue if you need help getting Genie alone, or later when you want everyone's attention. And good luck!" Flora smiled, genuinely happy for the pair. She had come to know Genie much better in the past months and had found the woman to be witty and generous, always seeing the best in people. The complete opposite of her sister Vivienne, in fact.

As if conjured by the thought, the first person Flora spied as she entered the Tearoom on the Rise ten minutes later was Viv Blanchette, along with Clive Langley, the village's new doctor. The man had only been in post for the past two months, as it had taken a while for the legal eviction notice to be observed on the surgery building which was owned by the Baker's Estate, and a suitable replacement found. The Edwards couple hadn't left Baker's Rise, however, instead deciding to flaunt their retirement to any who would listen. No matter that it had been imposed upon them because of Ernest Edwards' shocking neglect towards his patients and his attempt to press his advances onto Phil Drayford's late girlfriend last autumn.

Unfortunately, Phil himself was into his fifth month touring the world in an attempt to "find himself" and so without his vociferous reminders, public dislike for the Edwards couple had diminished as new gossip took their place. It would be fair to say, though, that the villagers merely tolerated the pair now, and they had certainly lost the status and revere they had once enjoyed in Baker's Rise. It was less that the villagers had forgiven and forgotten, and more that they were simply biding their time to find a legitimate, legal reason which would enable them to oust the couple from the community.

Despite the short time that he had been in Baker's Rise, the new doctor seemed to have his feet firmly under the table where Viv was concerned. Like two peas in a pod, one was rarely seen without the other, so much so that he had even hired the Blanchette sister as his receptionist at the surgery. This fact alone had put many of the villagers' backs up, as Viv was prone to gatekeeping the surgery as if it were a military base, refusing entry to all but life and death situations. As such, the doctor had very few patients and was not generally trusted by the locals.

Rumour abounded as to what he and Viv did all day holed up in the office, which was the exact opposite of what the parish council had hoped when they approved the man's application. Flora in particular had sought someone who would fit seamlessly and unremarkably into village life, with no question as to their character or motivations.

Seeing the pair together now, clearly taking a long lunch, their hands entwined on the table top, Flora's hackles rose once more.

"Viv, Clive," Flora said in acknowledgment as she sailed past towards Tanya at the counter, barely sparing the couple a glance. Adam, too, got a strange vibe off the man – or so he had told Flora – and on seeing the doctor took a sharp left turn into the bookshop.

Reggie seemed to agree, and followed quickly behind, merely shouting "Secrets and Lies!" as if as a foreboding.

Of what, though, Flora had no idea.

FOUR

Flora nodded and smiled, nodded and smiled as Tanya told her yet again how excited she was to be dressing up as Marilyn Monroe for the murder mystery evening. The fact that this particular starlet was neither Italian, related to Italian culture, nor a famous detective, as per the invitation, was neither here nor there according to the Ukrainian, as she detailed how she was about to get her hair dyed peroxide blonde and cut per the actress' signature style.

"You will look beautiful," Flora said, when finally the other woman paused for breath to put on her jacket, "and what is Pat coming as? I hope he can get the evening off work?"

"Well, ah, strictly speaking he is on shift, but he told

his boss at the station in Morpeth that he's required to provide police presence at a whole village function, similar to what he does at the summer fayre and they went for it! Just means he's coming as, well, a policeman, and P.D. Frank will be coming too!"

"Perfect," Flora replied absentmindedly, momentarily losing her train of thought as she watched Viv and Clive smooching two tables down.

"Eugh, they could at least get a room," Tanya said, following Flora's line of sight and refusing to lower her voice.

The loved-up couple must've heard, as they'd have had to be deaf not to, but the usually loud-mouthed Viv simply scowled in their direction. Not one to be cowed, Tanya scowled back until the arrival of Betty and Hilda was for once a refreshing break in the tension.

Tanya practically skipped out of the door on her way to the salon, and the older women received a well-timed "Ciao bella! Bellissima!" from Reggie, who had flown back into the room at the tinkling sound of the bell above the door.

Hilda blushed at what she considered a compliment, whispering to Betty that that meant beautiful and Betty herself told the bird to "Get off with ye!" Though Flora could see that she, too, was secretly pleased.

"I didn't know you spoke Italian, Hilda?" Flora asked as she took their order.

"My late husband, who was older than me, had served in Italy in the war, and he, ah, remembered some words that he then used back at home with me," Hilda was positively scarlet now and Flora smiled inwardly. She knew a lot about her neighbours, and yet every so often things would crop up that made her realise she only really saw the tip of the iceberg of their lives.

"I see the two lovebirds are making a nest in here today," Betty said loudly, breaking the moment.

"Well, I've not long arrived myself, but ah, yes, it would seem so," Flora replied, all three pairs of eyes on the doctor and his receptionist now.

"Aye well, love is a beautiful thing," Hilda said, clearly still deep in her memories as Betty tut-tutted at the pair earning her a "What?" from Viv, who grabbed Clive's hand and practically dragged him from his chair.

"Horrible smell in here," the Blanchette sister said as the couple left, staring pointedly at Betty and Hilda, for whom it was simply water off a duck's back. They were made of stronger stuff than to be intimidated or offended by cheap words, but Flora was annoyed on their behalf and calmly shouted, "Don't rush back," as the door slammed closed.

"All okay?" Adam asked, hurrying through at the sound of his wife's harsh words.

"Good riddance!" Reggie sat on the window sill, feeding off the atmosphere and hurling abuse at the retreating couple.

"It is now," Flora said, raising her eyebrows, but not wanting to rehash the whole episode.

"Perhaps you fancy sharing a pot of Earl Grey with two old ladies," Betty said to Adam, fluttering her eyelashes and causing the man to send a 'help me' look in Flora's direction.

"We'd love to," Flora replied, casting a small smirk that only her husband could see, "you can tell us all about your costumes!"

It was later that evening, back at the coach house after spending a tiring few hours up at the manor to oversee progress and to finish making and filling the cannoli with Genie, that Flora finally remembered to ask Adam whether the parcel containing their fancy dress clothes had arrived.

"Actually, it did," her husband said, looking very pleased with himself.

"And…" Flora was getting impatient.

"Why don't you guess?" Adam's flirty tone did nothing to curb Flora's growing annoyance. Nevertheless, he refused to simply divulge the information, so she was forced to play along.

"Antony and Cleopatra?"

"Nope, more recent."

"Romeo and Juliet?"

"They were teenagers!"

"Oh, okay, well, um…" Flora's mind went blank as she realised she didn't really know many Italian couples, "Come on, help me out."

"Okay, they are famous worldwide, with people of all ages."

"That's not very helpful, um, have they been on the big screen?"

"They have, and on smaller screens," Adam winked as

if giving away a huge clue, but Flora was still none the wiser.

"Vito and Mama Corleone from 'The Godfather'? If so, we might need a change of plan because I'm pretty sure Betty said that she and Harry are…"

"No, no it's not them. Come on, think outside the box, or inside it might be better…" He winked again, giving Flora the sudden urge to slap the man.

"I don't know Adam, if these are clues I've clearly never heard of the pair."

Sighing heavily, her husband produced a large package from under the kitchen table with a flourish and reached inside, "Ready?"

"More than ready," Flora's tone held no humour, even less as she saw what Adam produced with a loud, fake drumroll.

"Well?" he asked a few awkward moments later, as Flora's mouth was open in silent shock, her eyes wide and, he noticed, rather unforgiving, "You have to admit the caps are cute…"

"Cows loose!" Reggie squawked, trying to inject some humour into the uncomfortable moment, to no avail.

"It's Mario and Luigi... Super Mario Brothers from Mario Cart... the Nintendo game on Xbox and they just made it into an animated film and... or maybe I should have got you Princess Peach?" Adam tried to clarify, as if the bright blue dungarees and signature green and red shirts weren't a giveaway.

"Adammm!" Flora's angry growl caused Reggie to hide his face under his wing as if to say, 'You're on your own now, mate!' and made the man in question take a couple of steps back. His wife clearly needed a few moments to calm down and, well, get her head around the idea, he thought to himself as Adam decided there and then that a walk into the village would be a very prudent idea.

FIVE

For once there were no storms, no unexpected arrivals or unwanted surprises on the day of the Baker's Rise Murder Mystery evening, which was probably a first in the history of village events. Flora closed the tearoom and bookshop at lunchtime to go up to the big house. She had originally factored in a couple of hours to do her hair and makeup but since that was no longer required – a fact for which her husband was still suffering – Flora instead spent the time chatting with the actors, filling the last few cannoli and laughing with Genie about the housekeeper's costume. It seemed that she and Reverend Cartwright had decided to come as the Pope and a nun, and only now did it occur to her that that could be considered a bit inappropriate. Knowing what she did about the man's intentions for the evening, Flora did have a small chuckle as she envisioned the Pope getting down on bended knee to a woman who would ordinarily be found in a convent, but of course she let nothing of the surprise slip to her friend.

It wasn't until much later in the afternoon, only shortly before the event was due to begin, in fact, that things started to unravel slightly, giving Flora and Adam a definite sense of unease. They certainly made a striking pair, answering the grand main door at The Rise as two characters from a popular computer game, and all three might have had a chuckle about it, had Christopher Cartwright not turned up an hour early with his face paler than the white robes he wore.

He was greeted with a rather untimely "Sleep with the fishes!" from Reggie, who had indeed been watching too many Godfather films with Harry in recent weeks. The vicar brushed off Flora's attempt to apologise as she shooed the bird back to the function room where he was meant to be surveying proceedings from his perch, adorned with two trays of seed in the hopes of distracting the parrot from the buffet that would appear later in the evening.

"Christopher? Is that you? I thought you were coming

at six thirty to help with the welcome drinks?" Genie asked, joining them in the hallway.

"Well, I ah, I was hoping to have a word with Adam before it all kicks off. Nothing serious, love."

The housekeeper didn't look convinced, and to be honest neither was Flora, though she said nothing, assuming that the vicar wanted to keep whatever it was secret from his soon to be fiancée. If it was to do with the upcoming proposal, however, the man must have a heady dose of nerves judging by the pallor of his skin, Flora thought as she guided him into the study which was the only downstairs room not bedecked in Italian themed décor. Genie left them to check everything over one final time, and Flora was about to leave the room as well when Cartwright specifically asked if she too would stay.

"Oh, of course," Flora sat on the large desk chair, opposite the men who both looked rather squished on the cushy sofa.

"I got another," the vicar spoke straight to the point without prelude.

"A letter?" Flora gasped, "So soon?"

"Indeed," he replied, his eyebrows drawn and

forehead creased in much the same way as her own husband's current expression.

"Anything different? Any indication of the intended recipient?" Adam asked, flicking straight into detective mode.

"No, same musty old envelope, same smudged ink addressed simply to 'The Vicar', same notepaper. Only thing different is the actual message."

"Which is?" Adam's voice was low and quiet.

Cartwright produced the offensive missive from a pocket concealed in his Pope's robes, wrapped in a protective sandwich bag this time per Adam's instructions the previous day, and read through the plastic,

Tre, Due, Uno ... the clock is ticking down for you.

"I don't understand," Adam said.

"It's 'Three, two, one' in Italian," Cartwright clarified, "I looked it up. Do you think it's referring to tonight's Italian evening?"

"I hope not!" Flora exclaimed, "We're only expecting one – very fake, I might add – murder tonight. We certainly don't want a real…"

"Flora, sweetheart, I think you may be jumping the gun a little," Adam interjected, "understandable given everything that's gone on in the village in recent years, but still, I don't think our friend here needs to be thinking the worst."

"Oh, well, of course not," Flora said quietly, though the desire to retort with a petulant remark was strong and she clasped her hands together tightly to contain her unwarranted annoyance.

"Do you think I should still attend?" The vicar asked, his face positively ashen now.

"The whole village will be up here, you're much safer in company than alone at the vicarage," Adam clarified, "I'll ask Pat Hughes to keep a close eye on you and anyone that may be showing a particular interest in your location, and he can report back to McArthur if there's any suspicious activity."

Adam's confident plan reassured them all, and as Genie popped her head round the door asking if they wanted a cuppa, her boyfriend actually managed a smile.

"It would be a shame to postpone your… plans," Flora said, aiming for discretion.

"I know, and I, I won't let it," Cartwright said resolutely, "the show must go on as they say." He stood slowly and made his way to help Genie in the kitchen, oblivious to the worried glance which his hosts shared.

"People will start arriving soon, I'd better just check in with the caterers," Flora began just as her mobile phone started ringing in her dungarees pocket. She had to admit, these oversized overalls were great for carrying all your bits and pieces. Her humour was short-lived, however, when Flora heard Shona's anxious voice on the other end of the line. Whilst they were friends, Flora and the pub landlady rarely shared calls or texts that weren't related to village events. Certainly, they weren't on the level of sharing personal confidences.

"Who is it?" Adam whispered, putting his ear next to the phone which was held to the side of Flora's face.

"Shona, and she sounds upset," Flora whispered, shielding the device from her words with her other hand.

"Flora, I'm so sorry to bother you, but is Adam there?" The other woman spoke thickly, as if through tears.

"He is, I'll pass you over now," Flora replied, before shielding the mobile phone again and whispering, "You're popular tonight," to her husband. More to calm her own anxiety with a poor attempt at humour than anything else.

Of course, Flora could only hear one side of the conversation, and Adam wasn't the most talkative conversationalist at the best of times. So, frustratingly, she was none the wiser by the time he hung up, only able to tell by her husband's expression that all was not well at The Bun in the Oven.

"Well?" Flora prompted.

"Ah, well, it seems that Will is on the warpath and Shona is worried what he'll do. She's asked me to have a word with him when they get here. Only trouble is, they're dressing up as a gondola, with the blow up canoe around them, and the top halves of their bodies poking out as gondolier and tourist. Which is to say, they're literally joined at the hip, so you'll have to strike up a loud conversation with Shona whilst I chat to Will."

"Sweet natured Will? I've never heard him so much as

raise his voice, except that time at the summer fayre a couple of years back when he was angry with Shona's dad in the beer tent… Sorry? Did you say a gondola?" Flora wasn't sure which sounded more ridiculous to be honest – the idea of the village's placid vet being so angry as to be gunning for someone, or the nature of their joint costume.

"Aye well, turns out that pain he's been suffering from for well over a month, after running the 'Witherham Wanderers 10K' and taking a bit of a tumble, was actually a hairline fracture in his pelvis. He finally went and got checked out at the hospital in Morpeth today, after being put off by Dr. Langley who wrote it off as sciatica for weeks. Will should've been keeping all the weight off it, now his recovery time will be extended…"

"Oh my goodness! But he's already had quite a few days off work with the pain, lost some clients… he must be livid!" Flora's stomach sank at the thought of the upcoming showdown, "And surely he doesn't want to be coming to a party? And surrounded by an inflatable gondola of all things?"

"Well, Shona says the hospital gave him stronger painkillers, and says it's almost fused back together now anyway. The man's determined not to ruin her night out, since they've got a babysitter for Aaron and everything, as well as the fact he knows the doc will be here, so…" Adam raised his hands in a gesture of defeat, "I guess they're better here, where there'll be lots of police handy to intervene if needs be…"

Flora didn't like the sound of that. Not one bit. With a man of the cloth receiving threatening messages and one of the locals out for an unpleasant confrontation, Flora's only thought was *Mamma mia! Off we go again!*

SIX

As guests started to arrive, poking good-natured fun at each other's costumes, Flora felt the effects of the glass of red wine she'd just downed and managed to force herself to relax.

"Is there something inside your mouth, in your cheeks, Harry?" Flora asked, looking at her friend's altered features and noting that he looked rather like a chipmunk.

"It's cotton wool," Betty replied in a deadpan tone, "he's taking his role as The Godfather very seriously."

Flora swallowed down the snort that threatened to erupt, and turned to welcome the next visitors, an immediate frown forming when she saw that it was the Edwards couple. She had sent the invitation out of British civility and as dictated by politeness, hoping they would see it for what it was and decline. She should have known better though – Edwina would not miss an opportunity to try to reclaim the limelight.

"I'm Maria Callas," the woman in question said loudly, preening, "famous opera singer."

"She wasn't even Italian," Jean piped up from beside the drinks table, "I, on the other hand, am Sophia Loren, who most definitely was." None of the villagers allowed the disgraced doctor's wife to throw her weight around nowadays.

"And I am a white lily, national symbol of Italy," the usually shy Hilda May even did a little twirl of her charity-shop-find, 1970s wedding dress, trailing on the floor as it was far too long for her petite frame, and sporting a high, lace neckline which made the older woman look like a much brighter version of a background character in 'Little House on the Prairie', bolstered as she was by two glasses of sweet sherry in quick succession.

"And Dr. Edwards here is the best Italian racing driver ever, Alberto Ascari," Edwina had activated her selective hearing, that by necessity had been well honed since the autumn fayre.

"He's no longer a doctor, at least, not one that's fit for purpose," Betty piped up, grabbing another cannoli from a plate that was being handed around, "these little canteens are lovely, especially the lemon-filled ones, seems like they're popular too!"

Flora watched as Lily and Stan – covered in Italian flags which Lily had hand-sewn onto their farming overalls – took two each of the sweet treats to go with their coffees.

"Cannoli," Jean corrected, but Betty had her mouth too full to reply.

Then came Amy and Gareth in a similar inflatable outfit to the one Shona had described she and Will would be wearing, though theirs was a Ferrari, and next Laurie and Rosa in co-ordinating jumpsuits adorned with hand-embroidered, three dimensional spaghetti on one and meatballs on the other.

The imagination and trouble that her friends had gone to warmed Flora's heart and she had almost buried the feelings of worry until the next ring on the doorbell revealed Vivienne Blanchette and Dr. Clive Langley, dressed as none other than the Pope and a nun.

"What the?" Flora let slip before she plastered her hostess smile back on her face and welcomed them both as warmly as she could manage.

"Oh no," Genie whispered, coming into the main drawing room with more cups of coffee and tea for the guests who didn't want alcohol.

"How did she know?" Flora asked the housekeeper from the corner of her mouth as Viv floated into the busy room as if she didn't have a care in the world.

"She asked me outright! I never imagined it was so she could steal my idea. She came round here the other day to check I'd ticked everything off the organisational list for this evening – she hasn't lifted a hand herself, I might add – and saying she wanted to rebuild bridges, sisterly bonds and all that… I was stupid to believe her yet again," Genie looked so disappointed, so world weary in that moment, that Flora took the tray from her and suggested the shocked sister should go and find Reverend Christopher, who was in the kitchen with Adam, Pat Hughes and the two detectives. She presumed Adam had had enough time to bring them up to speed, and Genie looked like she needed the vicar's supportive arm around her.

A couple of minutes later, the detectives in question entered the main drawing room. It was the first time

Flora had seen their outfits as Adam had let his former colleagues in through the back door, and Flora couldn't hide her surprise. Timpson was clearly Sherlock Holmes – a look which actually seemed to suit the slight, shy young man well despite his being swamped by the cape and deerstalker – but McArthur seemed to be a giant fish, complete with full body scales and wide tail, and Flora couldn't quite see the connection to the evening's theme.

"The Codfather," McArthur answered her hostess's quizzical smile and even followed it up with a quick giggle, the first time Flora recalled the detective having expressed such mirth during their acquaintance, but then she was officially off duty for the night and had no need to keep up her professional persona.

"Ah, of course," Flora laughed politely and offered them drinks and appetizers, which were mainly half-empty plates of cannoli at this point, the villagers having devoured most of the sweet offerings. In fact, she noted, only those filled with coffee crème seemed to be left, the lemon, salted caramel and pistachio filled parcels all having been snaffled. Well, her guests would have to wait till the main buffet now, which was savoury pasta and pizzas and which wouldn't be served until the murder mystery troupe had performed their first two scenes. Of course, canapés themselves were usually savoury, but apparently not in Baker's Rise, as Flora had been sternly informed by Betty earlier in the week.

Flora had little time to contemplate the disappearing delicacies, however, as the bell went again and she had only a moment to be thankful for the grand, wide wooden doors of the manor house before she was flattened against the hallway wall by a rather large and cumbersome inflatable gondola. Will and Shona seemed to have already exchanged harsh words and to have achieved a distinctly uncomfortable silent standoff by the time of their arrival, huffing and puffing their way into the drawing room as they had been forced by their outfit to walk up from the village rather than drive.

"Please help yourselves to a drink and cannoli," Flora raised her voice to be heard over the hubbub, her words intended for the newest arrivals, but actually causing both Hilda May and Betty to reach for another drink and mini confection.

Of course, Reggie was in his element. He was certainly not going to let such an auspicious night pass by without setting himself up firmly as the star of the show. Stay in the function room with the actors? Pah! The feisty parrot had no such intention, and insisted on sitting on Flora's shoulder as she answered the door, choosing his favourite inappropriate welcome for whichever unfortunate was next. Echoing Flora, who caught herself saying "Mamma mia!" under her breath rather too often in that first half hour, the little bird now repeated the phrase with gusto, along with "Make him an offer he can't refuse!" and "Revenge is a dish best served cold!" which Flora was sure the little guy must have picked up from Harry's dubious film choice. Thankfully, he had yet to say "Sleep with the fishes" again, and Flora supposed that at this point she should be grateful for small mercies.

SEVEN

With the cast assembled and their throats well oiled, Flora gave the signal that they should all move into the function room for the First Act.

"What is this? The case of the three popes?" Edwina asked scornfully as they all gathered in front of the actors who had assumed their opening positions. The white robes of that immediately recognisable Roman pontiff could be seen on one of the actors as well of course as on Dr. Langley and Reverend Cartwright. A small snigger went around the room, and Flora simply shrugged her shoulders and gratefully accepted a glass of red from Adam. Beside her, Tanya was striking in Marilyn's signature white halter neck, floaty dress and stilettos, her blonde hair newly coiffed, though Pat was not with her. Presumably, or at least Flora hoped anyway, he was keeping a close eye on the vicar without arousing Genie's suspicions. Flora wanted her housekeeper to have a stress-free evening now that she had clocked off for the night, hopefully ending in the surprise proposal which Cartwright had planned.

In true Baker's Rise fashion, it was all going so well… until it wasn't. The audience huddled around the mystery cast, hanging on their words and desperate to pick up on any clues which might be dropped into the conversation. Some – the Edwards couple – were even so keen as to be scribbling in a notebook, obviously hoping to be the first to solve the murder later in the evening. As large as the room was, it was well filled to the extent that Flora had no idea if everyone was present in the space. It did cross her mind to check for any stragglers, and to perhaps retreat to the cool calm of the kitchen to liaise one final time with the caterers.

The mystery troupe were currently staging an argument between the character of the Pope and some kind of Italian council official, so Flora thought it the perfect time to slip out. Indeed, she had just whispered her intent to Adam when another argument, decidedly louder and more aggressive, broke out from the direction of the hallway behind them, causing all assembled to swiftly turn away from the main action of the evening.

"I'll deal with it," Adam said, already pushing his way back out. McArthur followed swiftly on his heels, though Flora noticed that Timpson was yet to move, and he himself was scribbling in his official notebook, immersed in the evening's entertainment.

"Shouldn't you be going with your colleague, lad?" Flora heard Lily say, though her tone was kindly.

"What? Oh! Yes, I was just, I mean I'm Sherlock…" the poor man stumbled over his words as he dragged his attention away from the acting on which it had been solely focused and back to the room at large, "Oh my goodness, yes, I hear what you mean." He too then hurried towards the room's only door, the crowd parting to let him through.

Flora took advantage of the open channel and also darted behind the young man, entering the hallway to find Shona physically restraining Will in their gondola, whilst Doctor Langley scoffed at them both for being "country hicks who wouldn't know medical skill if it reversed their obvious lobotomy."

"I'm a veterinarian!" Will roared, launching himself – and so his wife too – forward towards the man who simply leapt out of his way.

Three detectives (one retired) and a local bobby all tried to intervene in the restricted space until there was an almighty bang and Flora worried that a gun might have gone off. On the plus side, it brought an immediate silence to the scene and even the crowd pushing and shoving to get a good gawk from the doorway fell quiet and still. There was a shrill, whining sound as of an extremely large balloon deflating, which was the first indication that no one had actually been shot and it was in fact the gondola losing its air having been burst. Flora couldn't say she was disappointed to say goodbye to the cumbersome addition to the evening and forced a smile as she suggested those involved in the altercation retreat to her study whilst the majority enjoyed the rest of this first rehearsed scene.

Despite most of the villagers seeming more keen to follow the dispute between their neighbours than the actual mystery entertainment, Tanya assured Flora she would restore order, as Flora joined Adam and McArthur, Will and Shona, Clive and Viv.

"Shut up and listen!" Tanya could be heard yelling as Flora closed the door behind her, already feeling annoyed with Will and the doctor for the disruption they had caused.

"Do you have any idea how much this burst monstrosity cost?" Shona snarled at Viv, and it was clear there was no love lost between the two women.

As per usual, the Blanchette sister riled her neighbour up further by smirking smugly and slipping her arm through that of her newly-religious, papal boyfriend. "Possessions are worthless in the eyes of the Lord," Viv said piously, playing on her character as a nun.

"Oh, clear off," Will snapped, his eyes fierce as he tried to untangle himself and Shona from the plastic remains of their costume. Finally stepping out, somewhat gingerly due to his damaged joint, Will turned the full force of his anger on Langley, "You're a quack and a charlatan. How you managed to persuade them to hire you here, I have no idea, but I for one am looking into filing a legal claim. A complaint has already been lodged with the NHS..."

Will paused for breath and Adam took this as his opportunity to try to pour oil on troubled waters, "I can understand how angry you are, mate, really I can. If that had happened to me when I was still working... well, let's just say I didn't have a single sick day in all my years in the force so I can understand your frustration at having that forced on you."

"It's affected the trust the local farmers have in me, it's had a huge knock on my income, and that's before you even mention the physical pain and the stress it's put Shona here under…" Will was speaking fast, his face red and his fists balled. He was answering Adam, but his eyes never left the doctor's.

"Ignore him," Langley spoke up, his gaze fastened on Adam's, "he likely broke the bone recently and he's just looking for an excuse to sue me. The medical field is becoming a litigious nightmare, and good, honest folk like me have to navigate the maze with these chancers."

"Why you..!" Will attempted to launch himself towards the heavy, white robes of the man opposite.

Flora noted that McArthur had subtly positioned herself between Shona and Viv, while Adam was standing alongside Will, ready to grab him if things kicked off again. Which happened to be right about now, actually. Flora watched her husband lay a strong warning hand on the vet's arm, as McArthur whispered a word of caution to Shona to not credit the accusation with a reply at this point.

"Shall we have a drink and talk about it?" Flora suggested, knowing it was probably a futile request under the circumstances, "Or is it best for you all to avoid each other for the rest of the evening?" Perhaps talking about it now would only add further fuel to the fire.

"Actually, given the state of our costume and the way things have taken a turn, I, ah, I think it best if we just go home," Shona's bottom lip wobbled and McArthur kindly put her arm around the landlady's shoulders.

"What? No! I'm not letting him win!" Will bellowed, but Shona and the detective were already leaving the room.

"Ciao bella!" Reggie squawked from his usual perch in the corner of the room, from where he had overseen proceedings at a safe distance. Filling the uncomfortable moment which followed, in which the only other sound was Will's ragged breathing, the little parrot added hopefully, "Bananas per favore."

"You're nothing if not a trier, are you Reggie?" Flora said softly, coming over to join the bird as Adam had a whispered word with Will. Viv and Clive had left the room after Shona, no doubt to go and annoy someone else.

Sinking onto the sofa with Reggie on her arm, the wreckage of the flat gondola like a slippery rug on the floor in front of her, Flora once again questioned her decision to give the Blanchette sisters the evening they had pushed for back when she had first met them. Not Genie of course, she had turned out to be a gentle and easy-going soul, but Viv? Well, there was a character Flora was none the richer for being acquainted with. The fake candlestick on the mantle caught Flora's attention and for the first time in a long while she thought of the hidden office just on the other side of the opposite wall.

This house goes from the sublime to the absurd, Flora thought to herself, *and the people currently in it, well, even more so!*

EIGHT

When Flora and Adam finally emerged from the study some ten minutes or so after the village vet, having taken the opportunity for a quick breather and a debrief, it was to find the guests all assembled back in the function room, where the second rehearsed scene of the evening had just been performed by the cast of actors. According to the schedule, it was time for the audience to consider who might be about to be murdered and why, whilst enjoying the buffet of Italian food.

So far a silent observer, mainly of the meat pizzas in the kitchen to be honest, Frank the police dog now followed the catering team through to the drawing room where the food was to be laid out on the long sideboard beneath the bay window. Jean and Rosa had each provided a beautifully embroidered tablecloth – one in green and one in red – and Flora had divided the two with a vintage piece of lace-edged, white linen which she had found in the manor house during the big clearout.

Just as the group were about to descend on the food, however, the familiar sound of cutlery tinkling against glass announced that someone wished to have everyone's attention. Startled, Flora was incensed when she saw it was Viv who was about to launch into a speech, cue cards and all. Indeed, the woman had the gall to take credit for every part of the evening from the initial idea to the cardboard cutouts of famous Italian landmarks which decorated the main rooms. She mentioned her sister Genie only in the sense of the housekeeper carrying out the instructions she was given, no thought or participation involved. The woman failed completely to mention Flora's role in any of it, either as lady of the manor and hostess, or as equal organiser.

Seeing his wife becoming more and more enraged with every sentence that was uttered, Adam lay what he hoped was a calming hand on her shoulder. Not wanting to be pacified, Flora shrugged him off, unsettling the parrot on her other shoulder in the process. The little bird took to flight screeching, "Cows Loose! Sleep with the fishes!" For once, though, Reggie's antics barely registered in Flora's conscious thought, plotting as she was how to bring the awful woman down a peg or three. Righteous indignation flooded her veins as Flora thought how not just herself, but Genie too had been sidelined. Her housekeeper had gone bright red and had her head bowed, whilst Reverend Christopher looked like he was having some decidedly ungodly and violent thoughts on Genie's behalf.

"And of course, I couldn't have done it all without my Clive, an undeniable blessing and asset both to myself and the village…" Viv clearly hadn't read the room as she continued with her pre-prepared speech.

"Asset? I couldn't even get in to talk about my varicose veins last week, and the week before he didn't examine my bunions for more than a brief moment," Betty piped up.

"We reap what we sow," Edwina replied in her haughtiest manner – the one that made Flora want to slap her, "if my Ernest here were still village doctor…"

"Reap what we sow indeed," Tanya nodded her head, "you'd know all about that, Edwina!"

"The food is getting cold! Tuck in!" Jean raised her voice above them all, earning her a glare from Viv and a sigh of relief from everyone else who made an immediate beeline for the pizzas and pasta.

"Well, that could've gone better," Detective Timpson said to Flora as he passed on his way to the buffet line, "barely anyone was listening to the poor woman."

Flora knew the young man had no idea of village politics, nor of the true engineers of the evening's events, but his comment made her silent seething ramp up a notch. So much so that she had to slip away to the kitchen to cool down by the back door. She nodded to Pat who was outside on the gravel at the side of the house, muttering to Frank about pepperoni and diarrhoea, not that Flora imagined the dog could understand a word of it. In fact, he seemed quite content with the large piece of pizza he had in a vice-like grip between his gnashers, refusing to give it up to his master for love nor kibble. *No doubt took his opportunity when we were listening to that infernal speech,* Flora thought to herself.

Flora knew that the guests were about to be surprised after the meal with a scene set in the hallway and not in the function room as expected – it had been well rehearsed of course, but to the observers it would look like the impromptu discovery of a murder victim. Thus when the shouts that a dead body had been found began to filter down the corridor, Flora at first ignored them, knowing as she did that a member of the audience was meant to find the fake crime scene. It was only when she heard McArthur's voice sternly telling everyone to take a step back that Flora thought it might be wise to check in on everything. Not that she thought she ought to, of course, it being all Viv's event to take care of after all – *let that woman check on it!* – but she was still the owner of the house and there did seem to be a lot of commotion…

"Step away from the Pope…" In any other situation it may have seemed comical, farcical even, especially since the one giving the orders was a giant fish, but given that the man lay prostrate on her cold, Victorian tiles, Flora knew there was no humour to be found. Adam was ushering the onlookers back into the drawing room, without much success as half stood discussing the finding as if it were still a game and the other half were in abject shock and horror at the sight of white robes sprawled out carelessly before them.

"Ah, but which Pope is it?" Timpson said, rather tactlessly Flora thought, leaving her unsure whether the detective knew the body was real or not. Someone had had the good thinking to cover the poor deceased's face with his white zucchetto, so she too was wondering as to their identity, given there were three possible pontiffs.

For Flora herself, having been witness to the aftermath of too many murders now, she knew from the way McArthur and Adam were protecting the crime scene having checked the body for signs of life, that this was an all too real event.

"It's not Christopher Cartwright, is it?" Flora asked Adam, horrified at the thought that the gentle mannered vicar, about to propose to the love of his life, might have had his own life snuffed out.

"How could it be? Pat's watching him," Adam replied, his tone filled with the formality of his former profession.

"Oh! No, I actually just saw him outside with Frank."

"What? Well, where is the vicar? He could be in danger."

"Do you think this was foul play then? It couldn't just be a heart attack or something?" Even as she said it, Flora saw the telltale red seeping through the white robes below the deceased's head.

"Unfortunately definitely a crime involved, I would say," McArthur answered, stepping over to join them. She had tasked Timpson with the job of keeping all the guests in the drawing room, and Flora didn't envy him the role.

"So, is it the actor or the doctor?" Flora asked, for clarification, but realising after she voiced the question that it sounded like a line from a game of Cluedo.

"It appears that Doctor Langley has been hit on the head by a blunt force object causing loss of life," McArthur stated without emotion.

It was very unfortunate that at that very moment Vivienne Blanchette appeared from the direction of the downstairs bathroom, clearly hearing every word the detective had said.

"No! It can't be!" She shrieked. Although standing behind the woman, who had gone straight over to the body, Flora could see Viv's face in the giant ornate mirror that was hung on the opposite wall, as she clawed at her chest and screamed, "How could this have happened?"

"Ah, something hard and heavy to the head," Timpson

said, emerging from the sitting room and replying with about as much tact as an elephant.

"Hard and heavy?" Viv parroted back, no doubt in shock.

"Hard and heavy!" Reggie confirmed back to her, obviously thinking this was some sort of new game.

"Back to the front room," McArthur chased her colleague away sternly as if he were a child having crept down to see the grown-ups after bedtime. Timpson followed the order without question.

"Did you find the weapon?" Flora whispered to Adam as Viv screamed and sobbed on her knees at their feet. Genie had been drawn by her sister's cries and now had her arm around the trembling woman, trying to persuade her into the kitchen for some sweet tea to calm her nerves. Reverend Cartwright, too, had tried to help the distraught Viv only to be sent away by her wrathful abuse.

"Not yet," Adam replied, "we're going to need to question everyone. Get more hands up here from the station to do that and to search the whole property – inside and out – for the murder weapon. Then there's forensics, of course and the van from the morgue…"

He and McArthur sprang into action then, making phone calls and rallying the troops. Reluctantly, Flora joined her guests in the sitting room, anticipating an onslaught of questions.

Mamma mia! She thought to herself, *Off we really do go again.*

NINE

"You will need a doctor to sign the death certificate and ascertain cause," the moment he heard the sad news from Flora – who had opted to tell the group as a whole rather than repeating herself umpteen times – Edwards jumped up from the velvet sofa he had been sharing with his wife, Betty and Jean. Whether he saw this as an opportunity to ingratiate himself back into the affections of the villagers, or was simply keen to get away from the gossiping women, Flora wasn't sure, but she didn't stop him from leaving the room. *Let Adam deal with the man,* she thought.

After asking Timpson to go to the function room and explain to the actors that they weren't required to perform the rest of their scenes, Flora turned to the task of keeping the villagers calm and quiet until the uniformed officers arrived to take their statements. In good old Baker's Rise fashion, this would of course involve hot drinks and snacks. Despite having just demolished the buffet food like a flock of vultures, some had already begun muttering about the lack of refreshments, with Betty going so far as to ask if Flora had "any more of those little cannulas."

"It's cannoli, Betty," Jean had replied, clearly becoming exasperated.

"Aye, that's what I said. The lemon ones are my favourites," Betty nodded at Flora as if by way of sending her back to the kitchen to retrieve said sweet treats.

"I'll have to have a look," Flora said, actually relieved to have a reason to leave the stuffy room. Harry had taken his role as Vito Corleone extremely seriously and was currently puffing away on a disgusting smelling cigar, whilst Timpson had earlier been doing the same from his own character's tobacco pipe. Add that to sweaty bodies in cheap, unbreathable fabrics, the sickly plastic smell from the inflatable Ferrari which Amy and Gareth still wore, and the scent of strong garlic, and it was enough to make Flora feel decidedly queasy. That and the sight of the dead body as she passed by on her way to the kitchen, of course.

The spacious and airy room at the back of the house was sadly not the refuge it usually was, as Flora entered the kitchen to find Viv Blanchette still wailing like a banshee whilst her sister tried in vain to comfort her.

"Sorry to interrupt, just putting the kettle on," Flora said quickly, hurrying over to the counter under the window.

"It's your fault!" Viv screamed, as if suddenly becoming aware of Flora's presence.

"Excuse me?" Flora span around to face the two women who were sitting at the farmhouse table in the middle of the room. She felt a small amount of pity for Viv, who looked suddenly frail, wringing her hands so hard that Flora could see purplish bruises down her fingers.

"Aren't you meant to be head of the parish council, lady of the damned manor? It was your job to make the villagers accept him!" The woman railed and ranted, at the unfairness of life, at the evil lurking in Baker's Rise, at the fact it should've been her sister's paramour instead of her own…

To be honest, after the initial desire to defend herself had passed, Flora tuned the woman out. It was simply grief speaking and Viv no doubt needed to get it out of her system. Genie clearly shared her view, leaving the table and joining Flora at the worktop to set out mugs for coffee, cups and saucers for tea, and plates for the few dozen cannoli that had been kept in the fridge to sell in the tearoom during the week. As Flora began ferrying the trays back to the sitting room, enlisting Jean and Tanya to help her, she asked Betty to keep an eye on Hilda May who was back on the sherry and twirling around the room, tripping over her long white dress and singing 'Nessun Dorma' loudly and remarkably in tune.

For a little parrot who was normally outspoken, Reggie did a good job of keeping his beak shut as the evening turned into night and The Rise was flooded by police investigators. Too tired and stomachs too full to complain any longer, the villagers resigned themselves to the long, uncomfortable inquisition which followed, finding a few hours kip where they could and generally leaving Flora in peace.

Not that she felt much peace. None at all, in fact. Having eventually retreated to the master bedroom on the first floor, which she and Adam had decorated in advance of moving into the manor house when their first foster child arrived, Flora lay on the king sized bed with eyes wide open and brain whirring. At intervals, she could hear Edwina Edwards barking orders both to the uniformed officers and to the villagers, and for once Flora was content to let her. The whole build up to the event and then the evening itself had taken it out of her, and Flora felt completely depleted.

She stroked the face and wings of the little bird who snuggled under her chin, grateful for the reassuring warmth of his soft body. Reggie himself acted like Christmas had come early – Flora all to himself in bed with no Adam shooing him back to his cage on the landing? Perfection! All it needed was a fruit salad and it would feel like heaven!

"My Flora! Love you! So cosy!" he cooed happily.

"Umhm," Flora replied, having no energy to form a sentence. She had given a lengthy statement to McArthur, made easier by the fact the detective herself had been at the scene all evening and had been able to both make her own observations and corroborate her hostess's. Of course, Adam had also flipped the switch back into detective mode, and McArthur welcomed his help despite him no longer being allowed to contribute in a professional capacity. Flora suspected this was likely due to McArthur's lack of confidence in her new partner, with Timpson having been relegated to questioning the village W.I. ladies who mainly asked him for more cups of tea and complained about the lack of suitable entertainment.

It must've been at least three in the morning by the time Adam joined her, after McArthur had given the guests permission to leave the house, but not the village, and he had checked that Genie was safely to her room and the whole house locked up. He had also asked Reverend Cartwright to stay in one of the few spare rooms that was furnished, with a bed and nightstand, cuddly toys and children's books ready for a new arrival. Adam was worried for the vicar's safety – had raised it with McArthur in fact, that given the threatening notes he was surprised the good vicar hadn't been the victim – and felt for the man, who had had his hopes of a romantic proposal dashed by the tragic way that the evening had unfolded. Everyone else, though – Vivienne included – had been asked to go home, with the grieving woman transported back to the Blanchette house by patrol car.

"Get out of it! Stupid jerk! The fool has arrived!" Reggie let out a tirade of abuse towards Adam, whom he normally got along well with.

Flora had no patience for the outburst and repeated Tanya's usual line of "Desist silly bird!" whilst simultaneously yawning loudly.

"You need to get out of the silly dungarees, love, it can't be comfortable to sleep like that," Adam said gently, helping Flora up off the bed.

"It was a disaster, wasn't it?" Flora whispered as she searched in the chest of drawers for some light pyjamas, "They'll all want their money back."

"No, they won't, the ticket sales were for charity, weren't they?" Adam reassured her, though he himself didn't seem too convinced.

This was Baker's Rise, after all. The villagers may have generosity of spirit, but their purses were quite another matter!

TEN

Flora woke the next morning to rain pelting on the windows and a distinct chill in the room. "Well, this is summer in northeast England," she grumbled to herself, feeling the effects of too little sleep and too much anxiety.

Adam was noticeably absent from the room, as was Reggie, and the silence was eery, playing on Flora's lingering fears from bad dreams. Pulling on her dressing gown, she hurried downstairs to find the forensics team finishing up in the hallway, Timpson wandering around the rose garden looking for goodness knows what clues – his Sherlock Holmes' magnifying glass held to his eye and his deerstalker at a jaunty angle – and McArthur and Adam having coffee in the kitchen whilst Genie prepared a fried breakfast for everyone.

"Ciao bella!" Reggie squawked happily from the table beside them, green grape skin stuck to the side of his beak and a few slices of banana squashed protectively under his talons.

"I see you and Adam are best friends again," Flora said, ruffling the top of his head.

"Fickle, that's what he is," Adam said good humouredly as he pulled out the pine chair beside him for Flora to sit on.

"Any updates?" Flora asked, silently wishing she'd thought to get dressed before coming down.

"Still no murder weapon, cause of death confirmed as blunt force trauma to the head as we suspected, no other obvious injuries, some good leads to follow up on from the statements," McArthur listed quickly, "seems no one other than the wailing girlfriend liked the deceased, so we'll have to narrow down the list of suspects sharpish." Given her line of work, the seasoned detective clearly had a spare change of clothes in her car at all times.

"Why was everyone allowed to leave, when the

murderer was probably amongst the guests?" Genie asked from where she was busy at the hob.

"Because anyone could've come and gone at any point – all the doors were left unlocked and people were milling about on the front lawns and in the rose garden anyway," Adam replied.

"Well, unless the murderer hid it in their costume, or threw it in a bush outside, the tool or whatever it is must be here somewhere," Genie said, taking the teapot to refill as Timpson entered through the back door, "though admittedly there's hundreds of places they could've hidden it."

"It's a bit wet out there," the young detective said, stating the obvious as he wiped his wet face on one of Flora's best tea towels.

"No kidding," McArthur replied, though Adam took pity on the young man and suggested he go to the main bathroom on the first floor to dry off properly and then come down to have some breakfast with them.

"We all have to start somewhere," he said to McArthur after Timpson had left the room and the detective merely grunted in reply.

"When we've had this I'll get on with de-Italying the place," Genie said, handing Flora a full cup of Earl Grey just the way she liked it.

"I'll help," Flora forced a smile, "that'll be okay, won't it detective? To start dismantling the cheesy paraphernalia?"

"Should be, just shout if you find anything noteworthy."

"Will do," Flora agreed, though it felt like every bone in her body protested the thought of another physical activity. What she craved now was a deep bubble bath and a book. No talk of murders or weapons or…

"I am so sorry I slept in," Christopher Cartwright appeared in the doorway looking as dishevelled as Flora knew she must too. Still dressed in his pontiff's robes, the vicar had dark grey bags under his eyes and his hair was sticking out at odd angles.

Genie gave the man a look of pure, unadulterated love and walked over to give him a hug – the first time Flora had seen them embrace in public. It was so wholesome and sweet, it reminded Flora that, despite the several unfortunate brushes with murder she had encountered, there was still goodness to be found around every corner. *Such a shame he wasn't able to pop the question,* she thought, *hardly a romantic setting with half of the Northumberland police force descending on the place.*

"I should go and see Viv," Genie said quietly, all joy gone from her features now as she passed around plates and brought dishes brimming with bacon, eggs, sausages and fried mushrooms to the table, though her tone suggested she'd rather have her fingernails removed than visit her sister.

"I'll come with you," the vicar said immediately, standing to grab the plate of toast that the housekeeper was balancing on her forearm, though his voice too held more than a hint of trepidation.

"Probably not a good idea, but thanks," Genie said, finally sitting down herself.

"I'll be going down to The Bun In The Oven to make sure Will and Shona were back there when the murder happened, given the confrontation between the vet and the doctor earlier in the evening. Though I actually have no idea how we'll be able to confirm it since it seemed the whole village was up here. There aren't likely to have been any witnesses as apparently they'd even closed the pub for the evening, perhaps the babysitter…" McArthur said around a mouthful of buttered toast.

"Oh, I saw him chatting with the acting troupe when I went in to tell them their services were no longer required," Timpson said, entering the room at that moment.

"Wh-wh-what?" McArthur spluttered as she choked on the bread, causing Adam to give her a sharp slap on the back, "Will? You mean Will Monkhouse, as in the local vet? That's who you saw?" So incredulous was she that this was the first time her partner had mentioned such an important piece of information that McArthur stood hastily, scraping her chair against the tiled floor, her face bright red. There she stood, hands on hips, her eyes blazing an angry path straight to Timpson's.

To give the man his due, he met her stare for stare, not cowering backwards under the force of it which Flora knew she herself would've done.

Picking up on the sudden tension, Reggie screeched "I'm all shook up!" and made a beeline through the small open door to the right and down into the comfort of the laundry room, where he often enjoyed a snooze on the clothes horse.

"Did he say why he'd come back up the hill?" Adam asked in an even tone, though Flora could tell from the small muscle twitching beside her husband's left eye that he too was displeased to be learning this information now and not last night.

"Forgot something apparently," Timpson said nonchalantly, taking a seat and helping himself to three rashers of bacon. Either he was so obtuse as to not understand why this news was making his colleague annoyed, or the man simply didn't care. *Maybe a bit of both*, Flora thought, and not for the first time she silently questioned what had prompted the young man to enter the profession in the first place.

McArthur too sat back down, though more slowly, the anger evident in the hard set of her jaw. She gulped back the remainder of her coffee and pushed her still half-full plate away before returning abruptly to her feet and barking the order, "Right Timpson, no time for breakfast, we need to get to the pub."

"Aye, I'll follow you down," Adam added, unable to resist joining the investigative team.

Thankfully having the wisdom to present no protest, the young man grabbed two slices of toast, shoved his bacon in between them to form a sandwich, thanked Genie and Flora for the hospitality and followed his partner out.

"Well, that's not a match made in heaven," the vicar said drily, and Flora was inclined to agree.

ELEVEN

After taking a quick shower and dressing in the first pair of trousers and linen blouse she came to in her wardrobe of surplus clothes that were kept up here at The Rise, Flora joined Genie in the front sitting room where the carnage from the night before was even worse than she had feared.

The empty plates and dishes were still strewn over the buffet table, as last night the police had asked that everything remain where it was. Stacking them up ready to be carried into the kitchen, Flora discovered that her beautiful white tablecloth now had "Hilda was here!" scrawled in messy writing, in what looked like pink lipstick, and surrounded by a wobbly heart.

Partly shocked, partly amused at how drunk her usually staid and shy neighbour had become, Flora hoped the thick marks would come off in the wash. It did remind her of the notes the vicar had received though, and she took a moment to pray that he wouldn't arrive back at the vicarage to find another on the doormat.

Pat and Frank had turned up at the manor house half an hour earlier to escort the man in question back to the church, keen to perform the duty that they had neglected for part of the previous evening. The policeman had been rebuked by McArthur shortly after the murder, despite his protests that his canine companion had been unusually belligerent, and Pat had seemed keen to make amends. When Genie had asked for the reason behind such a necessity as escorting her boyfriend home, Pat had blamed it on the dog, saying that Frank needed some fresh air and a long walk after some rather unpleasant bowel movements that morning. That was too much information for everyone, and had the desired effect of nipping the housekeeper's questioning in the bud.

Cutlery, napkins, drinks glasses, cups, saucers and mugs littered the room, along with the discarded remnants of costumes. Flora had actually borrowed extra crockery and utensils from the church hall, and so was worried that some might have become chipped in the general kerfuffle. Thankfully, all seemed to have come out unscathed, save for two white mugs which appeared to have smudged blue dye on them. Even scrubbing with neat washing up liquid failed to remove the blotches which stood out on the white china, and so Flora decided just to bin them. She and Genie had far too much to do to worry about trivialities.

When the front room was all cleared up, the dishwasher filled with the first load, and the items that required handwashing drying on the drainer by the sink, Flora suggested they take the weight off their feet before tackling the function room and hallway. Lunchtime had been and gone as the two women worked, all of the remaining crime scene staff had left, and a small green parrot's chirps were becoming increasingly demanding as he realised his seed bowls had not been refilled since breakfast time. Such shocking neglect!

"I'll make us some sandwiches," Genie said wearily, standing slowly as if the effort pained her.

"No, you sit down, you made us all breakfast," Flora urged her friend back down onto the chair, "I'll make them and a pot of Earl Grey, and after we've eaten you get yourself along to Viv's and I'll see to the rest of the rooms. They shouldn't be as bad as the drawing room anyway. Besides, Adam will be back from helping McArthur in the village soon so he can lend a hand."

"Only if you're sure," Genie hid a yawn behind her hand, "though I'm, ah, not sure if I can face her today, I might telephone first to see how the land lies."

"Good thinking, but if I might risk speaking out of turn," Flora paused and Genie nodded, "please don't let your sister take out her grief on you, Genie. She can be… harsh at times, as you well know, and I'd hate to think of her making you feel bad about your own relationship with the vicar, or persuading you to move back in with her because she's going to be lonely."

"I won't, I won't" Genie said, but neither of them were convinced. It had taken her years to get out from under the wing of her overbearing sister, and had their mother not passed away suddenly the previous year Genie might well still be suffering there.

Flora had the radio on loudly to compensate for the unsettling silence in the house after Genie retreated to her own room, the housekeeper promising to give the place a good dust and polish before the day was done.

Flora was working methodically, along the entrance foyer and hallway and then into the large function room, taking down Italian flag bunting, flattening the cardboard statues of the colosseum, Vesuvius and Trevi fountain. It was as she went to lift the leaning tower of Pisa, which stood in the corner just inside the doorway of the function room, that Flora let out a loud curse.

"The blummin thing weighs a ton!" She told Reggie, who eyed her from the high curtain pole, his head tilted as if he was judging her weakness.

Flora tried again, her knees bent and chin down this time. Still she could not lift the stupid box high enough to carry it against her torso.

"But it's meant to be hollow cardboard like the others, and they were light as a feather," Flora muttered, standing straight and trying to stretch out her protesting muscles.

"What is?"

Flora jumped at the voice right beside her ear and glared at her husband who held his hands up in apology.

"Sorry, love, sorry, the radio was on so you mustn't

have heard me come in."

"Well, it's perfect timing, because apparently I'm a weakling," Flora snapped, pointing at the offending decoration.

Her husband flashed Flora a confident smile, before putting his hands around the bottom of the box and lifting it fully. Had his upper lip not erupted in droplets of sweat and his breath faltered, Flora might have thought he found the task easy. As it was, the item clearly weighed more than even Adam had envisaged.

"Goodness me, what did you weigh this down with, love? Rocks?"

"Weigh down? Why nothing. All the landmarks stood upright without any trouble and I figured it would be safer if people didn't stub their toes against them. Come to think of it, I deliberately didn't leave any in the doorway like this for that very reason," Flora searched her memory for the exact location of the leaning tower before the guests had arrived, "this one was way over there, beside the floor lamp."

Although he was still listening to her, Adam had now lowered the box gingerly back to the floor and was examining it closely. When he whipped his mobile phone out of his pocket and began taking photos, Flora knew the former detective was onto something. Leaning forward and squinting she saw the smudges of red, stark against the black and white background now that she was aware of them.

"If my guess is correct, there will indeed be rocks or even bricks in the bottom of this," Adam said sombrely. I imagine whoever had it in for Langley stood hidden in this doorway and then whacked him on the back of the head with the tower as he passed by, their strength fuelled by adrenaline. They would've had to act fast, no time to think twice, in case they were spotted by the acting troupe. Since that cast have all been questioned and none saw a thing, I would say the murderer had more luck than good judgement. Obviously the act was premeditated, since they filled and moved the cardboard decoration, but the moment itself seems to have been very impulsive and risky."

"Oh my goodness," Flora's hand covered her mouth in shock at their discovery. She hoped she hadn't destroyed any potential evidence by grappling with the tower before Adam arrived, but that couldn't be helped now.

They had found the murder weapon, hidden in plain sight.

TWELVE

The discovery necessitated a call to McArthur and resulted in the investigating team descending on the manor house en masse again. Genie was asked to come down for another round of questioning, though the poor woman had no recollection of the leaning tower decoration other than that she had helped Flora to unfold and fasten the large boxes and place them all in position the other day, at which point she was certain they had all been able to be easily lifted. Flora clocked the red, swollen eyes and blotchy face of her housekeeper but made no comment, given as they were in the busy drawing room. Instead, at the earliest opportunity, she asked kindly if Genie could make some tea for everyone, giving the woman a chance to disappear to the much cooler and calmer kitchen.

"Ooh, you sexy beast! You're a corker!" Reggie squawked at a female officer who was examining all of the other, now flattened, cardboard landmarks for any unusual markings or fillings. She was crouched down in the corner of the large room and had shrieked when the green parrot landed on her head. Not perturbed, Reggie had made his way to the woman's shoulder by way of sliding down her face, and was now assailing the new object of his affections with his choicest words of endearment.

Flora had no energy to walk across and remove the bird, so simply raised her voice and said, "Reggie! Leave her alone!"

Apparently affronted by the order, the parrot gave Flora a side-eyed glare of pure disgust, and levelled her with the title "You stupid old trout!"

This, at least, caused the young officer to giggle, and Flora decided to let the woman deal with Reggie herself. Of course, the bird took the laughter as a sign that his attentions were welcomed and so continued with his dubious courting technique.

After taking a call from Tanya, who had been in charge

of the tearoom for the day and who was reporting back that the village ladies were disgruntled at the lack of available information on the previous night's crime, Flora joined McArthur, Timpson and Adam in the function room. This large space had originally served the house as both a formal dining room and a ballroom when required, and it would have been the responsibility of the manor house's numerous servants to adjust the room's purpose as required.

Although Flora had replaced the dingy, dark wood on the ceiling with a much brighter plaster and cornicing, and had had the room wallpapered in a light, floral design, she had kept several of the original features. These included two large, double-doored china cabinets which stood on either side of the deep fireplace – currently half empty as Genie was yet to refill them with the crockery used the previous evening – and two large bookcases at the two corners of that wall.

These consisted of six rows of in-built shelves and a back board which was attached to the wall itself and reached from floor to ceiling. Flora hadn't much bothered with them, to be honest, other than to have the house clearance company stack any books they found on the shelves. There they sat, no doubt gathering dust until Genie was employed as housekeeper, with Flora having it on her list to ask Harry if he wanted any but never actually getting around to it. They weren't the kind of thing she sold at the bookshop, or even stocked in the little library corner, being mainly on the topics of hunting, fishing, gambling and drinking.

"I just don't understand what the murderer did after committing the crime," McArthur was saying, "I mean, there's one door to this room, and they would've been hidden in the shadows of it, maybe behind the velvet curtain at the window which ends just there, so that they wouldn't be seen by the acting group. So, they jump out, they see the long, white robes, they do the deed and then what? Do they stay in the hallway where they can be spotted? Walk nonchalantly back into the drawing room on the opposite side, stepping over the body? Or even simply raise the call and pretend to have just found the victim?"

"I'd say the first two are too risky, especially since they must've planned where to put the leaning tower, and the third, well, it was Hilda May who literally tripped over Langley in her drunken state, so I don't think she'd have been compos mentis enough to carry out such an orchestrated act. Apart from the fact I doubt she could've even lifted the tower," Adam replied, "No, I would hazard they re-entered this room, but then what? Where could they go, quickly and quietly as all hell broke out in the hallway?"

All four pondered this question, but none could think of a plausible explanation.

"So, what did Will say when you questioned him?" Flora asked the group to fill the silence, her curiosity getting the better of her.

"He admitted to being back up here. Couldn't not tell us really, since Timpson had seen him, but he did try to fob us off with a forgotten coat or something." McArthur explained.

"Aye, until I reminded him he didn't have a coat, just a shirt and neck scarf per the gondolier he was portraying," Adam said, sounding pleased with himself.

"So then the man had no option but to confess," Timpson added.

"Confess?" Flora's high pitched voice conveyed her shock. She wanted this all solved quickly, of course, but Will? She couldn't believe it.

"Not to the murder," McArthur clarified quickly, tutting at her partner for his ambiguity, "Monkhouse admitted that he'd asked the actors to change the end of the night's script. So that when the big reveal happened, and they were meant to accuse one of their own, they would instead point the finger at Dr. Langley."

"I think he just wanted the man embarrassed and humiliated," Adam added, "Will had asked them to accuse Langley of having killed the victim by accident, because he was such a bad doctor, and for this to be announced to the whole village. To discredit him and hopefully make him rethink his position in Baker's Rise."

"The group have given a statement to this effect too, and we've said they can leave the village, but of course it could all still be a ruse by the vet. A cover which allowed him to re-enter this room and begin a conversation after committing the murder. It would explain the conundrum we were just contemplating…" McArthur looked thoughtful.

Before anyone could comment on this, however, there was a loud scraping sound, of wood grating against wood, and Timpson only managed to jump out of the way just in time before the shelves beside them began to move.

"What the..?" Adam shouted, as the whole bookcase appeared to swing slowly on unoiled side hinges and open into the room as a door.

"Adam!" The shriek was out before Flora could stop it, part fear, part shock.

A bundle of green feathers flew in from the normal door behind her and landed on Flora's shoulder, no doubt alerted by her tone.

"Mamma mia!" Reggie screeched, as a figure appeared in the darkness of the new doorway.

THIRTEEN

"Don't mind me, just putting away the last of the good china," Genie said, carrying a large tray of cups and saucers.

The four witnesses stood with mouths agape and moved to the side as the housekeeper went to the closest mahogany cabinet and set the tray down on the floor.

"Is everything alright?" Genie asked, as if she hadn't just appeared from a secret tunnel wearing a headtorch to guide her way.

"Secrets and Lies! Watch out! Hide it all!" Reggie screeched, flying off to safety back in the direction he had come.

"I, ah, what is..?" Flora began, but Adam and McArthur had already rushed through the doorway and so she felt compelled to follow them. The space smelt foisty, of decades-old dust and damp, but Flora could hear footsteps ahead and hurried after, not wanting to be alone in the enclosed, long unused space.

Using the flashlight on his phone, Adam climbed a small staircase at the end of the long, narrow corridor and emerged into the laundry room – into the walk-in linen closet, to be exact. What was now obviously a much more recently added, fake, plywood back to the ceiling-high cupboard, was placed carefully to the side, leaning against some shelving.

"Oh my goodness" Flora exclaimed, breathless.

The three moved into the laundry room proper to have more space, with Timpson notably absent.

"Sorry, claustrophobic," his voiced echoed through to them causing McArthur to roll her eyes.

A few moments later Genie joined them, blushing as if embarrassed to have caused such a commotion, "I hope you don't mind me using it? It's just a quicker shortcut with the heavy trays, you see, probably originally made for the servants to move about out of sight…" she worried her hands together making them too turn red.

"I don't mind at all," Flora said slowly, "but, ah, how did you even find it?"

"Oh! I assumed you already knew it was there," Genie said, "I was getting the ironing board out a couple of months ago and before I could get a proper hold on it, the metal end rest for the iron had tipped backwards and knocked the fake back wall a little out of place. I couldn't resist but see where it went. It took me a while to work out how to open the door at the other end though, at least until I used a strong enough torch…"

Flora couldn't quite believe what she was hearing. Indeed, had she not just walked through the proof herself, she might think she'd been transported back in time to a creepy, black and white suspense film, where she was in an old castle that was riddled with secret passages and chambers. An involuntary shiver passed through her.

"I take it you didn't know about it, Flora?" McArthur said, her voice wobbling slightly as if the detective were holding her emotions in check – whether excitement at the find or consternation, Flora couldn't tell.

"She would've told me if she did, wouldn't you love?" Adam added.

"I certainly didn't know it existed," Flora confirmed, "but I guess we now know how the murderer got out of the room undetected…"

All eyes were on Genie again, and there was a very pregnant pause.

"Have you ever told anyone about this shortcut?" McArthur asked, her eyes narrowed to slits.

"N-No," Genie stuttered, but even Flora got the impression her housekeeper was not telling the truth. She certainly caught the look that McArthur shot Adam confirming her own gut feeling.

"We'll need to have another little chat," McArthur told Genie, taking a gentle hold of the woman's elbow and directing her up the narrow stairs that led into the main kitchen.

The housekeeper stuck to her story during the questions which followed, with Flora hovering around pretending to wipe down the counters. Yes, it had been an innocent discovery, yes, she thought both Flora and Adam must already be aware of it, no she had not come across any other secret passageways, no she had not divulged this discovery to anyone. Over and over until the poor woman had her head in her hands and the usually timid Timpson spoke up to defend her.

"I think Miss Blanchette has been very forthcoming, very helpful with our enquiries, has she not?" He directed the question at McArthur but made no eye contact, that apparently being a step too far.

"Very well, show us the hidden handles to unlock the door at the function room end and that'll be enough – for now," McArthur said to Flora's relief. She couldn't believe for a moment that this kind-hearted woman who had moved into her home and looked after it, and her, with such great care could possibly be a murderer.

After Genie had shown them the spot to push on the back of the secret door from the inside of the hidden corridor – the wood rubbed shiny with use over the decades so quite obvious when one was standing right there – and then the same on the side of the function room, though this was a hidden panel under one of the shelves at waist height and right at the back beside the wall, the woman seemed quite overcome with exhaustion and emotion. McArthur suggested the housekeeper go to her room and have a lie down, though Flora suspected this were not a simple act of compassion but rather a way to both know where the suspect was and to continue the investigation without her overhearing. Regardless, she too encouraged Genie to take a rest and secretly wished she could also have a nap herself.

It was well after six before the house was once again quiet. McArthur had asked Flora for a list of anyone who may have known about the secret corridor, either recently or in years gone by. Once she thought closely on it, Flora realised that unfortunately she could never give a conclusive list, there being many villagers who had lived through Harold Baker's tenure at The Rise and even that of his parents. Plenty of people who could have been told about the servants' routes or been shown them in days gone by. As far as definitive names went, Flora sadly had only one – Genie.

There had been a distinct lack of fruits, seeds or indeed any decent snackage all afternoon, and it was a very disgruntled little parrot who Flora roused from his nap in the study to go back down to the coach house. It felt like weeks since she had been back in their cosy home, though Flora knew in reality it had only been yesterday. Not wanting to disturb Genie, who had her own set of keys, Adam locked up behind them. They had already given a spare key to McArthur, as Flora had no intention of hurrying up to let them in every time the detectives wanted to check one thing or have a second look at another. No, all she wanted was to get back to her routine in her tearoom and to look at booking a holiday somewhere warm and sunny… and with extremely low crime rates.

FOURTEEN

All signs of the previous day's downpour were gone and the conditions reverted back to signs of summer, as Flora and Adam walked down to open the tearoom the next morning. The brighter weather brought higher spirits and Flora felt her mood return to its normal, content state. It's a wonder what a long soak in the bath with lots of bubbles can do, especially followed by a meal cooked by your husband and an early night with no disruptions. Flora didn't feel completely like a new woman, but almost.

Reggie, too, was in high spirits and demonstrably happy when they continued straight along the path to the tearoom rather than turning left towards the manor house.

"Welcome to the tearoom," he squawked happily,

flying ahead and then looping back to Flora.

There was only one black cloud on the horizon – well, two if you counted the murderer still on the loose, but Flora wasn't quibbling over technicalities – and that was the effect a murder at The Rise would have on the couple's chance to be foster parents. They had already been approved a short while ago, and had been hoping to welcome a little person soon, but with this new tragedy in the very home they had prepared to bring a child into… Well, Flora could understand if that put a black mark against their application. She and Adam had spoken about it briefly the previous evening as soon as they got back to the coach house, but both had been tired and in an overly pessimistic mood. This had resulted in Flora becoming upset, them both jumping to the worst case scenario, and Adam asking if they could wait until today when they could actually speak to a social worker and get the facts rather than hypothesizing an outcome that may or may not happen. Of course, Adam's logical, rational suggestion had clashed with Flora's own emotional response, and it had taken the length of her bath time for them to both cool down and apologise. Nevertheless, they had gone to sleep on good terms, ready to make the important call today.

Adam therefore went straight into the empty bookshop

side of the building to phone their social services liaison in private, whilst Flora focused on the early birds who were waiting outside for her to open the café. It was Tanya's day off, as Flora had extended the tearoom hours to include all seven days now – as an experiment for this summer – and taken on Amy to help them out when necessary. Strictly speaking, Amy was still on maternity leave from the hairdresser's but she had handed in her notice when Flora offered her the job and said she could bring baby Barney to work with her. Amy had expressed a desire to work in the bookshop from before it was even opened, and so Flora had honoured her promise that the young woman would be given first refusal if a role came up.

So, it was just Flora who welcomed Reverend Cartwright and Hilda May into the coffee shop, wishing she had had a quieter first half hour to get everything set up.

"Visitors! Visitors with money!" Reggie chirped happily, perching in his usual spot and keeping a beady eye on Hilda's handbag, from which he knew the woman had the habit of producing a few fat blueberries, brought specially for him.

For once, the vicar didn't offer to share a table with the elderly woman, nor was he wearing his dog collar and black blazer, so Flora assumed the man must be off duty. She served Hilda her pot of Earl Grey and fruit scone and moved on quickly before the woman could get into the local gossip. Hilda looked put out that her hostess hadn't stopped by the table long enough to chat, so Flora made a mental note to spare her some time after she had spoken to Christopher.

"I'm so sorry your proposal plans were ruined the other night," Flora whispered as she sat down next to the vicar under the guise of fussing with the cafetière she had set on the table.

"Well, that's nothing compared to a life lost," Cartwright said desolately, "I just came to ask after Genie. She sent me a text late yesterday afternoon saying she'd been busy clearing up all day, had a migraine and needed some peace, so I haven't contacted her since. Perhaps she's angry with me, but I'm not sure why that would be. Maybe I wasn't supportive enough the other night? I was just a bit in shock, you see, seeing a mirror image of myself lying dead on the floor, after having received those worrying notes and all."

"Oh I hadn't thought of that, you and Langley both being dressed the same," Flora said kindly, "it must have been very strange seeing the body and the robes all laid out like that."

"It really was, and then the police split everyone up according to where they'd been at certain times, to question us all, and... well, I'm not sure I was there for Genie in the way that she might have wanted."

"I'm sure she's not cross," Flora said, though she felt awkward speaking on behalf of her friend whilst also trying not to divulge information that was crucial to the investigation, "perhaps just give her some space and try again in a day or two? It's true she was, ah, very busy yesterday."

The man opposite her nodded, but his expression was grim in the way of one who feels all hope of love is lost, and Flora empathised with him. Beyond that, though, her hands were tied.

Luckily at that moment Adam came through from the bookshop, looked as if he were about to signal to Flora to come and speak with him, but then got distracted by spotting Hilda May.

"Ah, Mrs. May, my colleague, ah former colleague that is, is looking for you. I believe you couldn't give a statement yesterday because you were indisposed?" *With a hangover* was the implication, but Adam had the tact to refrain from saying it.

"Oh!" Hilda blushed bright red, dropped her butter knife and looked to Flora for help.

"Do you still need to answer the police's questions, Hilda?" Flora asked gently, seeing Adam slip away again behind the woman, no doubt to call McArthur.

"Yes, I suppose so, though I don't think I can tell them anything," Hilda said defensively, "I really just came this morning to apologise, Flora, for ruining your special event."

"You didn't ruin it," Flora said, sitting down next to the anxious woman who was winding her fingers in knots in her hand-embroidered handkerchief, "a coldblooded murderer did that."

Mrs. May's complexion turned two shades paler, whilst Reverend Cartwright rose abruptly and left the tearoom without so much as a goodbye. Flora got the distinct impression she'd said something wrong.

"Yes well, I was… not in my normal frame of mind," Hilda whispered.

If 'not in your normal frame of mind' includes graffitiing tablecloths, dancing on furniture and tripping over dead bodies that are in plain sight, then indeed you weren't, Flora thought drily, but aloud she said simply, "It was certainly a night, wasn't it?"

"It really was," Hilda agreed, "and so good of you to get me a taxi home."

That 'taxi home' had been a police car, but the inebriated octogenarian had clearly been completely unaware of events going on around her.

Flora felt bad for the inquisition she knew was about to take place when the detectives arrived, but equally knew she would listen to every word. A bit like seeing a car crash but being unable to avert your eyes.

Yes, Flora thought to herself, *things are about to get interesting!*

FIFTEEN

"Nothing to worry about, Mrs. May, just a few questions," Timpson said kindly as he and McArthur joined Hilda at the table.

"You're a good lad," Hilda clasped the detective's forearm and squeezed, "you look just like my late husband did when we first wed, bless his soul."

Timpson blushed beetroot as Reggie added his own appreciation, "You sexy beast!"

McArthur was in no mood for such frivolities, though. Still wearing the same clothes as the previous day, the woman looked as if she hadn't slept either, "Right, let's just get on with it, shall we?"

Hilda immediately clamped her mouth shut and regarded the woman standing opposite her with apprehension, while Adam and Flora hovered behind the counter, hanging on every word as if it were a soap opera.

"Let's start at the beginning," McArthur said, "You had rather too many sherries and tripped over a dead body."

"What?" Hilda's hairy chin quivered and Flora felt sympathy for the older woman.

"Do you drink often, Mrs. May? Do you have a history of alcohol induced memory loss or foul play?"

"What?" Hilda asked again, looking to Timpson and then to Flora for support.

"What my collea… ah, the detective means," Adam said slowly and clearly, "is whether you often like a tipple in the evenings, when you're knitting maybe?"

"Oh, ah well, once a week when Yarn Wars is on I have a sweet sherry, yes. Helps to calm my nerves, the programme keeps me on the edge of my seat, you see," Hilda managed a wavering smile in Adam's direction, deliberately looking straight past McArthur who in that moment had the face of a bulldog chewing a wasp.

"I see," Adam said, pausing as if mulling that information over, "but the other night it's fair to say you imbibed quite a lot. Do you remember, Mrs. May? You were dancing and singing?"

Hilda May's face went from white to bright pink faster than you can say cherry pie. Clearly, the question triggered some sort of recall as she blinked quickly three times in succession and then stammered, "Oh my goodness!"

"And there we have it," McArthur said, taking the spare seat at Hilda's table, "thank you Bramble, I can take it from here."

"So, big white lump in the hallway, you went flying, right?" It was hardly a professional tone, but McArthur was clearly on her last nerve where the villagers were concerned right now.

"I, um, oh Lordy, yes, I was looking for more of those little sweet tubes, I was going to go to the kitchen and I almost fell on top of… Oh Sweet Mother Mary, somebody killed the Pope!" Hilda shrieked and buried her face in her handkerchief.

"No, no, not the real pope," Timpson reassured her, for once more sensitive than his partner, which was saying something, "remember, there were three of them. It was fancy dress, you were a banshee…"

"A banshee?" Hilda repeated with evident indignation, "I was a white lily! National symbol of France!"

"Italy," Flora corrected then clamped her mouth shut when she was on the receiving end of McArthur's glare.

"So you drank a lot and discovered the body," McArthur's jaw was clenched so tightly it was almost square.

"Yes, Betty Bentley had just told me, you see."

"About what?" Adam asked.

"About the letter from Yarn Wars, saying we've had our application accepted! They're coming to film in Baker's Rise later this year!"

"Mamma mia!" Flora groaned.

"Off we go again!" Reggie finished for her.

"Argh!" McArthur growled.

"I'll put the kettle on," Adam said, "it's going to be a long morning."

They had established that she was very drunk, that her actions were out of character, that she had discovered the body, and that she had shouted for help, mainly because the hem of her dress had become caught under the heavy weight of the deceased. Mrs. May then recalled being sick over the hydrangeas out front, possibly from the discovery, likely from the alcohol. She remembered dancing with a young policeman, or attempting to at least, and then waking up, several hours later on a bench beside the front lawn.

All of this had taken precisely two hours and thirty-three minutes to ascertain, during which there had luckily been no other customers at the Tearoom on the Rise. They had been through two pots of tea, three cafetières of coffee, two rounds of ham and chutney sandwiches, half a banana loaf and five cheese scones. McArthur had declared it the darkest day in her whole career and Reggie had treated the whole thing as an indoor picnic, hoovering up after them all with gusto.

It was as the two detectives were about to call it a day with Timpson being tasked with writing up the ramblings into some form – any form, in fact – of coherent statement for the witness to sign, that Hilda May blurted out, "Of course, there was the ghost."

"Ghost?" McArthur asked in a defeated tone, not even

pausing as she walked towards the door.

"Aye, the one that walked through the wall," Hilda said, as if pleased that her memory was returning.

Of course, after the previous day's discovery, the mention of people going into walls caught the detective's attention and McArthur hurried back to her seat.

"Tell me more about that," she said, her tone much more encouraging than at any other point that day.

"Well, before I tripped over the pope I had walked straight across from one main room to the other, instead of turning left towards the kitchen, silly me!" Hilda giggled, "That was when I saw the ghost disappearing into the wall. Then I went back out into the hallway, turned in the right direction that time and tripped over the pope. I shouted and Harry Bentley came to help me free my skirt and…"

"Woah, woah, woah," McArthur interrupted, "back up lady. Okay, so you cross the hallway, don't see the body because you're fixated on getting cannoli, walk into the function room and see… What? An actual person? A shadow?"

"Oh it was the full shape of a person, a woman

definitely, and she walked into the bookcase and disappeared," Hilda said, nodding her head vigorously.

McArthur shared looks with both Timpson and Adam, before continuing, "And this woman, what was she wearing?"

"Oh?" Hilda replied, as if she'd just been asked to recite the lyrics to a song she'd never heard, "Ah, well, it was a dress."

"Yes… Colour? Style? Did you see her face?"

"No just the body from the back as they disappeared. Do you think this means I'm haunted now? Oh, Flora, your house is haunted! You could charge for tours and investigations. I've seen that on the tele, you know…"

"Focus, please Mrs. May," McArthur was pleading now, just a small step from outright begging in fact, "What. Do. You. Remember. About. The. Ghost?"

"It was just like that black lady from the film with all the chasing and singing," Hilda May slammed her spectacles down on the table as a sign of a job well done, whilst her audience merely looked perplexed.

"Um, there were only a few black people at the event," Flora began, hoping she wasn't sounding racist, "the new school teacher Joy Fields and her husband, the Patels from Witherham, though strictly speaking they're more brown-skinned…" Flora clamped her mouth shut, not wanting to veer onto the tricky territory of exact skin colour.

"No, not black face, black dress! But the lady in the film had a black face!" Hilda exclaimed as if Flora was stupid to even think it.

"I've got it!" Timpson shouted, slapping his own hand on the table in glee, "She's talking about 'Sister Act'. The nuns singing and Whoopi Goldberg dressed as one. The ghost was dressed as a nun!"

SIXTEEN

They bundled Hilda out of the tearoom with all the politeness of a flock of Reggies, and then the two detectives, Flora, Adam and the parrot rushed up the hill to the manor house. Flora fumbled with the key, trying to lock up the café at such speed that she wouldn't be left behind. This wasn't about simple curiosity, no, she was determined to make sure her friend got a fair hearing. After all, they only had the word of a drunken pensioner to go on. That being said, things weren't looking good for Genie, not good at all.

McArthur had used her spare key for the back door and was through the kitchen before Flora caught up, huffing and puffing behind them. She had been skipping one too many Jazzercise classes and it was starting to show.

"Watch out! Hide it all!" Reggie warned as they all ignored the empty kitchen and made a beeline for the front drawing room. Finding that room also devoid of life, the two pairs split up, with Flora and Adam searching the rest of the downstairs and the two detectives taking the upstairs. Meeting back in the study several minutes later, all looking red faced and decidedly more dishevelled, it was to report that the manor house appeared to be empty.

"Right, let's check that secret corridor, and Timpson, you go and see if the housekeeper has emptied her wardrobe," McArthur spoke quickly, "Flora, just to confirm, that passageway is the only secret space you know about?"

Flora shot a look at Adam, which didn't go unnoticed by his former colleague. Reluctantly she moved to the mantle and pulled the fake candleholder to the side. The familiar grinding noise followed as the secret door slid open and revealed the small, neat office inside.

"Cool!" Timpson exclaimed, his eyes wide.

"Sleep with the fishes!" Reggie added from his perch by the window. No good ever came from this little room being opened.

"Well, that's a turnup for the books," McArthur's eyebrows were unnaturally high but her voice remained even, "and this is all?"

"Ah no, actually," Flora stepped inside, moved the rug and showed them the trapdoor, "it leads into the basement, and from there you can go through the external door to the patio at the back of the house."

McArthur's mouth widened into a momentary grin that even she couldn't control, "Very neat, very neat indeed," she said, before quickly flicking back to being all business, "Right, Timpson, you get down there, walk right through the cellars and come out the back. Adam, you and I will check out the servants' corridor, and Flora please check Genevieve's room to see if anything looks amiss or cleared out in haste."

Timpson looked like a schoolboy in a sweetshop as he disappeared into the bowels of the building, before Flora hurried off to her friend's bedroom. It certainly felt like an invasion of privacy, to be honest, but Flora knew they couldn't clear Genie's name if the woman herself wasn't present to do so. Certainly, it looked a lot worse for the housekeeper if she was nowhere to be found. Sitting on the bed, Flora tried to phone Genie, with the ring tone eventually going through to voicemail. She left what she hoped was a calm and not unduly worrying message, asking simply if all was well and making up a query about cutlery that she required an answer to. Then Flora left the same message via text and set about looking in the wardrobe and drawers. A quick glance was all she needed to see these were still full. What's more, Genie's reading glasses still sat on her nightstand along with her box of daily medications. Flora presumed anyone leaving – even suddenly – would remember to take their prescriptions with them.

"Right well, it's obvious she's done a runner. Maybe a tipoff, but from whom? Did she have an accomplice?" McArthur mused as the three sat around the kitchen table whilst Flora prepared a pot of tea.

"You don't have any of those cannoli left, do you?" Timpson asked, despite the veritable feast they'd eaten not so long ago in the tearoom.

"Ah, no, sorry," Flora heard herself snapping back and tried to soothe it with a half-smile. She really didn't like the turn things were taking but felt powerless to divert it.

"And what was her motive?" Adam asked, "Do you know, Flora, if Genie Blanchette knew Doctor Langley before he moved here? Or could she have been jealous of her sister's relationship with him?"

"I very much doubt it was jealousy," Flora spoke firmly, "Genie and Reverend Cartwright are in a committed relationship, as you know."

"You can never know with matters of the heart," Timpson said, as if he had all the dating and relationship experience of a man three times his age.

For once, McArthur agreed with him, "Yes, matters of the heart can be a strong motive. Right, sup up Timpson we need to organise a (wo)man hunt!"

Flora was sure she didn't like the glee in the detective's excited tone, but she held back her remark and showed them out through the back door.

"I wonder if she's not just visiting her sister as she'd planned to do?" Flora said to Adam as she sat back down, in what she felt was a moment of inspiration, "There could be absolutely nothing untoward or sinister at all about Genie not being here. Her hours are flexible, and she certainly deserves some time off after all the clearing up she did. I bet she's just gone visiting. Or the vicar? What if she's spending some time with Christopher?"

The look of envy that Adam had tried but failed to

hide as he watched his former colleagues rush off was replaced now with a thoughtful smile.

"Good thinking Mrs. Bramble-Miller, we'll make a detective of you yet! It does take a while to rally the troops and get a proper search going. I suppose there's no harm if in the meantime two villagers make a couple of informal visits, just neighbourly care really after such a tragic incident…"

"Absolutely," Flora smiled widely now and grabbed her handbag.

In their eagerness, they almost forgot the little parrot who was sound asleep on his perch in the study. Seeing the door to the secret office still open, Flora closed it, retrieved the bird who was all the more grumpy for having been disturbed, and hurried out after Adam, keen to get on with their plan.

SEVENTEEN

The Blanchette house stood at the end of the village, beyond the end of Cook's Row, down a lane and around the corner. It was almost hidden by a ridiculously overgrown privet hedge, so Adam had driven past the driveway before they realised their mistake. After dropping Reggie at the coach house, it had simply seemed quicker to bring the car.

"If we check this out, and the vicarage, then I can let McArthur know she can strike those two places off her list," Adam said happily as they parked up. The once-gravelled driveway was now more a carpet of weeds and the path to the front door looked no better.

"Unless we find Genie, then we'll have even better

news to report," Flora said hopefully, regretting wearing her new sandals.

They rang the doorbell, which seemed to make no sound so that the couple couldn't be sure it had rung inside the house either. Then they tried the rusted lion's head knocker. When still no response came, Adam attempted to make a sound with the letterbox, though that was too full of flyers and junk mail to be accessible for the purpose. Becoming exasperated, Flora began to shout up towards the two upstairs windows whilst Adam peered through the dirty glass of the only downstairs window. Still no luck.

In the end, a combination of doorbell, knocker and both shouting loudly attracted some signs of life within the house.

"Who is it? I don't like beggars," came the muffled reply from the other side of the peeling black door.

"It's Adam and Flora," Adam spoke up first, "come to check on you."

"In your horrendous grief," Flora added, hoping that would do the trick and play to the woman's narcissism.

Sure enough the sound of several bolts and chains being moved was followed by Vivienne Blanchette's face peering round through the narrow opening she had created, "I'm as well as can be expected," she said curtly, "since the love of my life was murdered at your infernal party."

Flora wanted to comment on how it was apparently her party now that it had all gone downhill, despite Viv having claimed all glory on the evening itself, but she simply smiled through gritted teeth and said "I'm so sorry, can we come in for a chat? I could make you a cuppa and…"

"No!" was the shouted response followed by a much calmer, "No, thank you, I seem to have come down with a virus and I wouldn't want to spread it."

The woman looked her usual sour self from what Flora could see, not even any tear tracks or blotchy cheeks to indicate she had been grieving. Adam stepped forwards as if to open the door further, but Viv grasped the side of it from the inside and held on tight causing him to retreat back again.

After a few moments of apparent standoff, Adam spoke gently, "Well, we'll be off then Miss Blanchette," and made as if to turn around. "Oh, just one more thing, you haven't seen your sister have you?" He looked back towards her nonchalantly.

"No, why?"

"Oh, I need to remind her to be, ah, up at the big house for a delivery," Flora fibbed.

"No, she hasn't been up here since she moved into your huge pile on the hill. And good riddance to her I say!" Viv said, slamming the door dramatically.

"Well, she's a charmer," Adam whispered as they walked away.

"Yep, with family like that, you wouldn't need enemies," Flora replied, and Adam nodded knowingly.

There was no long wait at the Vicarage, as the door was opened before Adam could even knock twice.

"Oh," the vicar said morosely, "I was hoping it might be Genie. Come on in then."

Flora and Adam shared a look but said nothing as they followed Reverend Cartwright into the gloom of the hallway. Unlike when the Marshall family were home, with seemingly every light on and noises aplenty, the place seemed to have been plunged into darkness. Flora wondered if the man had even bothered to open all the curtains.

"Come through to the kitchen, it's the only room I'm using apart from upstairs," the vicar said, leading the way.

Clearly parish duties had been forgotten along with the housekeeping, Flora thought as she entered the room that was full of dirty dishes, newspapers and books. Cartwright slumped down into the armchair in the far corner beside the French windows which opened out onto a pretty walled garden, leaving Flora and Adam to take seats at the kitchen table.

"So, what can I help you with?" The vicar asked, more than a hint of impatience to his voice.

"We just came to see if you've heard from Genie?" Flora said, before immediately wishing she'd been more subtle.

The man's expression became even more dejected as he replied, "No, she's clearly had enough of me. I've blown it, like I always do."

"I'm sure that's not the case, mate," Adam said, "she probably just needs time to ah, clear the decks and everything." Even Adam himself wasn't quite sure what he meant by that.

Not that it mattered, as the vicar had already caught onto Flora's subtext.

"Why are you looking for her? She's okay, isn't she?" He jumped up and paced towards them.

"Of course, of course," Flora was quick to reassure, "I just need to remind her to be in for a delivery that's all."

Dealing with people day in day out as part of his professional duties, Cartwright paused with eyes squinting at her, moving his weight from one leg to the other.

"Couldn't you text her, Flora?"

"She's ah, not replying, maybe her phone has lost charge," the suggestion came out more rushed than Flora had intended and she could feel sweat start to trickle down the back of her neck.

"She's not replying to me, either," Cartwright sat back down on the chair, though his eyes were more alert than when they had arrived, "What do you think, Adam, given the threatening messages I received? Could they have targeted Genie now? Have I put her in danger through association?"

Adam had not expected either this calculated reasoning or the vicar's logical conclusion. Knowing what he did however, he suspected Genie was not innocent in the whole situation and therefore preferred to believe she had taken herself off out of the village in an attempt to evade justice.

Of course, he couldn't explain any of this to the man opposite and so said, "No, you haven't had any more and there was no mention of Genie in the first two. I wouldn't worry."

Flora shot her husband a quick look as the vicar ran his hands over his corduroy-clad thighs and sighed heavily.

"Well, if there's no contact by tomorrow, I'll go up to the big house and demand she talk to me," Cartwright said decisively.

Since Adam suspected the team would have Genie in custody before then anyway, he nodded, "Good plan. Anyway, we'd best be off, there's probably a line outside the tearoom." The attempt at a joke fell flat, as it was already past closing time, and Adam himself planned to have a drink in the pub on the way home.

"Very well, thank you for coming," Cartwright said, the epitome of British politeness – thanking visitors that turned up unexpectedly, brought nothing, and who you couldn't wait to get out the door again.

EIGHTEEN

A small detour to The Bun In the Oven had been a mistake.

Given the impromptu early closure of the tearoom, and seeing an influx of police officers searching the village, the residents had all taken it upon themselves to visit the pub. It had nothing to do with hearing the latest gossip about the murder, of course, and all to do with supporting local business. Shona was rushed off her feet behind the bar and appeared to be well past the point of losing her temper, whilst the ladies of the village had pulled several tables together and were whispering in hushed tones.

"All clear, thanks Shona," Pat said appearing from the

door behind the bar with Frank.

"I don't know what you expected to find in my beer cellar," Shona snapped, "I could've told you there's nothing new down there. Haven't even taken a delivery since last week."

Pat raised his eyebrows, but in his usual good-natured way didn't respond. Instead he paused beside his wife on his way out, kissing her gently on the forehead. Tanya blushed and giggled, her Marilyn-esque blonde curls bobbing, as she watched the stout man leave, being dragged along by the energetic Alsatian.

"I think it might have been more of a who than a what," Betty said loudly, looking to Adam for confirmation.

He deliberately ignored her, facing the bar and waiting his turn to be served. Flora had found them a table at the other end of the room, away from their neighbours, where she hoped her husband wouldn't be plagued with queries.

"Hmm you might be right there," Tanya agreed, also casting her voice in the direction of the former detective.

"But who? I mean we all know the top suspect is

Will…" Betty stopped short, realising her mistake, but it was too late.

Shona paused in polishing the counter, which was so shiny you could see your reflection in it. She had ignored Adam and the other two customers in the queue before him, and had seemed to be cleaning rather aggressively as if on autopilot. That was, until she heard her husband's name.

Marching over to the table of ladies, hands on hips and a face like thunder, the landlady said, "My Will is innocent, as well you all know. Didn't you have a problem with the new doctor yourself, Betty? Couldn't it just as easily be you who did him in?"

"Why!" Betty exclaimed, but was drowned out by the sound of Shona's loud sob. Having finally reached her limit of stress for the week, she flew back behind the bar, out of the door, and they heard her quick footsteps on the old stairs leading to the flat above.

The whole place fell into awkward silence.

"Well, someone's a bit tetchy," Betty whispered, but she did have the grace to look remorseful.

A few long minutes later, Will clomped down the stairs, clearly not wanting to be out in public. He was wearing what looked to be pyjama bottoms with a stained t-shirt and unbrushed hair. Flora had never seen the man so ungroomed.

"Right what can I get you? Hurry up I don't have all day," he barked, to a few mumbles of discontent from the two men in front of Adam in the line, who had been waiting quietly and patiently for at least five minutes.

The vet served their pints in record time, with a record amount of froth on top too by the looks of things, but thankfully they just tutted and paid, glad for any drink under the circumstances. On looking up and seeing that Adam was the next customer, Will appeared first angry, then shocked, then seemed to whisper something before taking the order.

Flora heard her husband reply, "of course," before joining her at the table, her long awaited glass of red in his hand.

"What was all that about," she breathed against his ear, not wanting to fuel local hearsay any further.

"Will asked if he and Shona can come around later, when Aaron is in bed. They'll ask his mum to babysit again."

"Did he say why?"

"No, but I think we can imagine," Adam didn't look happy as he took a sip of his lager shandy – only a half pint as he was still to drive them home.

"It is a bit awkward, you having insider knowledge," Flora mused, "people will obviously want to take advantage of that."

"Well, you've benefitted yourself, once or twice," Adam smiled at her but Flora could tell the situation was far from ideal. She herself couldn't see how her husband could've refused the request, though, so it was a bit of a stalemate.

"I know, though it doesn't seem worth them coming round when the investigation has already moved elsewhere."

"Well exactly, but I could hardly say that to the man with the town tattlers within earshot," Adam jerked his head in the direction of the ladies. Flora caught Betty's eye as she turned slightly and gave her best innocent, nothing-to-see-here wave.

The door behind the women opened just as Will was about to escape back upstairs and the man sighed audibly. Flora was happy to see the new arrivals, though, and waved to Laurie and Rosa to come and join them. For once, her groundsman looked less than happy. Adam took their drinks order then braved the bar again, whilst the couple got settled on the worn faux leather banquette that ran along the wall under the windows.

"Is everything okay?" Flora asked after appropriate greetings were made.

"Si, si, just taking advantage of little Matias being with the childminder," Rosa said, casting a warning glance at her husband.

Laurie removed his flat cap and scraped his hand through his hair, as if in deliberation. The moments drew out and Flora was about to make conversation, when the gardener said, "Actually Flora, I hope you don't mind me saying, but it's getting a bit much actually!" He took a deep breath in, as if relieved to have voiced his concerns for once.

"In what way?" Flora asked, secretly shocked. This was the first she'd heard that the man wasn't happy.

"Well, first there was the Italian evening, and I got the gardens looking beautiful for that, only to find them the next morning having been littered by guests and trampled by police. Then, today, I go up to take delivery of those roses we ordered and get about planting them, only to see another horde of uniformed ants stomping all around the place again," Laurie's face was red from the embarrassment of speaking his mind and Rosa tapped him gently on the arm.

"Well, unfortunately we can't help the searches, mate, bit of a necessary evil under the circumstances," Adam said, getting back to the table in time to hear the groundsman's comments. Flora herself was grateful to not have to weigh in on any confrontation, though her sympathies did lie with her employee.

"I know, I know, but the extra work it's created is…" he sighed heavily and shrugged his shoulders, took a large sip of his pint of ale and was seemingly restored to equilibrium, simply happy to have got his point across, "Anyway, no matter, I've got all summer to give the place the attention it deserves. Just got myself a bit riled up about it, that's all."

"I'm so grateful for the way you work your green-fingered magic," Flora said, and meant it, "I know Billy would be so proud of how you've kept his favourite place looking great, all the plants thriving and flowers blooming."

Laurie's redness intensified as he blushed at the compliment and Rosa smiled widely and gave a nod of thanks to Flora for having silenced the metaphorical bee in her husband's bonnet.

"So, we were hoping to speak to you, and this may not be the best time," Rosa took a sip of her lemonade, "but perhaps it is, as I find it better to focus on the joys of life at times like this. So, with that being said…"

Both Flora and Adam leaned forwards in anticipation, grateful for any good news right now.

"…With that being said, would you be the godparents for our new arrival due later in the year?"

"Of course!" Flora squealed without hesitation, catching the attention of Betty and Tanya who both looked keen to know what had caused the outburst.

"Thank you, thank you so much," Laurie said, "we can't think of a better couple."

"It'll be an honour and a privilege," Adam added, visibly overcome with emotion. Flora knew her husband had never been asked to perform such a role before and it would mean a great deal to him.

"We're delighted!" Flora gushed, kissing Adam on the side of the head and jumping up to hug their friends.

"When all's said and done, life still goes on," Adam said as they left the pub half an hour later.

"And we have to grab it with both hands," agreed Flora, still buzzing from the invitation to be godmother.

Like Genie and Christopher, she thought, coming back down to earth somewhat as she remembered the outstanding accusations and the precarious position her housekeeper was currently in.

Little did Flora know how precarious…

NINETEEN

Flora opened the door to the coach house and let out a shriek as a cloud of feathers assailed her, "Reggie! Oh my goodness, so many feathers! He must be…"

"Calm down, love, these feathers are white. When I last looked, our parrot was green. And there he is, sitting looking at us from the top of the kitchen door, like the cat that got the cream."

"Or the bird that got the cushion," Flora said, frowning at their pet, who still had the empty cushion cover hanging from his beak, "and hasn't even bothered to hide the evidence! Reginald Parrot!"

Flora had known that the side seam from one of the decorative cushions on their bed had come undone and had meant to sew it back up, but needlework wasn't one of her favourite pastimes, to say the least, and it had never risen from the bottom of her To Do list. Seemingly, Reggie had saved her the job by pecking away at the hole and then flinging the thing around until all the feathers were freed from inside.

"Maybe he thought it was one of his relatives stuffed in there or something," Adam joked as he fetched the dustpan and brush.

"He's never normally destructive when I leave him," Flora mused, "something must've set him off."

"Well, his seed tray's empty," Adam said, spotting the small bowl which had also been flung onto the floor in apparent disgust, "if anything would rile the bird up, that would."

"Is that it?" Flora directed the question at the parrot, "You surely can't be hungry, though." Flora picked up the plastic container and took it into the kitchen, making no comment as the cushion cover was dropped onto her head from above.

Seeing her reach into the cupboard for the bag of seed, Reggie flew down onto Flora's shoulder, all having apparently been forgiven, "My Flora! She's a keeper!" He squawked happily.

"Yes, well, it's a good job I love you," Flora whispered.

"Love you!" Reggie parroted back at her, making Flora feel warm and fuzzy inside.

"He's got you wrapped around his little beak," Adam smiled as he tipped the half-floating contents of the dustpan into the bin.

Having dealt with that rather unexpected welcome home, and now snuggled on the sofa in the small sitting room with two big mugs of tea, Flora finally found the courage to ask what they hadn't had a private moment to discuss until now.

"So, ah, you managed to get through to the social services team this morning?" She chewed the inside of her cheek anxiously.

"I did, love, and there wasn't much to report, or I would've mentioned it straight away. I spoke to a nice woman who said there isn't really a precedent for whether they'll place children in buildings where a murder has recently occurred. She said she'd have to do some investigating of her own and get back to us, but she suspected it may hang on whether the murderer is behind bars and what the recommendation of the detective in charge of the case would be. So I gave her McArthur's number and she said she'll get back to me when she knows more." He put his arm around Flora's shoulder and pulled her close, as much for his own comfort as his wife's.

"I guess there's nothing we can do but wait, then," Flora replied morosely.

"Aye love, I'm sure when the time's right we'll…" He was interrupted by the doorbell and the subsequent shrieks of a little parrot who was angry at having his meal disturbed.

"Get out of it! Somebody else! Stupid git!"

"Reggie!" Flora tapped a warning finger on the bird's beak as Adam went to answer the door.

"Hope we're not disturbing you…" Flora heard Shona's voice and went into the hallway to welcome the couple.

"Not at all," Adam replied, "come in, I'll pop the kettle back on and you have a seat in the living room with Flora."

Shona's blotchy face still bore the evidence of her earlier tears as she sat on the settee with Flora, whilst Will took the armchair opposite. Flora rubbed her friend's arm wordlessly and eyed Reggie with her sternest warning look.

Ignoring her, the little bird scanned the visitors, did a double take when he spotted Will, and began shrieking "Not the vet! Not the vet!"

"Quiet or cage!" Flora warned, getting a beak full of seed husks launched in her direction in return.

"Ah Reggie, we're friends, aren't we?" Will said, his tone soft and conciliatory.

"The fool has arrived!" Reggie gave his final decision, clocked Flora about to stand up and remove him from the room, and made the wise decision to hide his head under his wing in long-suffering silence.

"We don't want to disturb your evening," Will said when they all had hot drinks and a plate of jammy dodgers had been passed around, "and I know you're limited, Adam, in what you can tell us, but…"

Adam interrupted him then, "Actually, I can confirm the case has moved in a different direction. I know your mam vouched for you getting back to the pub when you said you did, and then getting her a taxi home as her babysitting duties had ended early, so that gave you an alibi anyway, perhaps a shaky one since you were seen back up at the big house afterwards, but since then more evidence has come to light that points elsewhere."

"Really? Oh my goodness," Will let out a huge sigh of relief and looked like he might cry.

Shona couldn't hold back her own tears, the result of over a month of pent-up stress, and Flora took the cup from her shaking hands and passed it to Adam so that she could comfort her friend.

"So it's all o-over, for W-Will, for us?" Shona stammered.

"Can't say that till they've caught the killer – and in any case it's no longer my place to say at all," Adam replied gently, "but off the record, yes, I'd say it's all over where you're both concerned. You can relax now and Will here can focus on getting that fracture fully healed."

"Ah thanks mate," Will stood carefully and shook Adam's hand as the women hugged, "been the worst month of my life this has."

"Well, I know it's not easy, but in my experience you need to draw a mental line and move on," Adam said, "the police aren't in the way of giving apologies and the bloke to blame for your undue pain and stress is no longer around, so nothing to do but get on with life, eh?"

"Absolutely," Will said, "and we'll get going and leave you in peace." He looked a different man to the one who had arrived fifteen minutes before, "next time you're in the pub the drinks are on the house!"

Peeping out from under his wing feathers to check the couple were actually getting on their way, Reggie chanced a quick "Good Riddance!" quickly stuffing his head back under before Flora could say anything.

"Well, at least that's someone who's happier," Flora said as they returned to the sofa having seen their guests out, "I can't help thinking about Genie. She didn't take anything with her. How will she eat or put a roof above her head?"

"Well, she'll have a bank card in her purse I presume, for the account that you pay her wages into, which McArthur will be having traced. So, hopefully the woman will stop for those things and they can catch her before she moves on." Adam spoke so matter-of-factly it made Flora mad.

"But there isn't even any proof yet!" She raised her voice, angry with the situation more than her husband, "Nobody has even been able to question her! I'm sure Genie could explain it all. And as for wanting to kill a man just because your sister is finally happy as McArthur suggested, well that's a pretty thin motive if you ask me!"

"A lot of circumstantial evidence, I agree, but then there's Mrs. May's statement about the nun and the hole in the wall…" Adam's voice was even as he tried to explain his former colleague's thinking.

"Let's not go through it all again," Flora snapped, "I just hope Genie is okay. She's still my friend, Adam."

"I know, love, I know, and when they find her you can be sure she'll be treated fairly and allowed to have her say," he opened his arms and Flora walked into her husband's embrace.

"Life isn't fair," Flora whispered through the lump in her throat. She knew she sounded childish, but it wasn't just the murder, it was her dashed hopes for becoming a foster parent in the near future too.

"Aye love, I know, I know," Adam ran his hand over her hair and kissed the top of Flora's head, "we just have to make the best of it."

TWENTY

Flora had just come out of the bath and dressed in a lightweight dressing gown over summer pyjamas when there was a hammering at the coach house door. Thankfully Adam was still dressed and reading in the sitting room with Reggie snoozing on his chest, so Flora hid back in the bedroom and let her husband answer the door to their late visitor.

"Get out of it!" Reggie squawked, disgruntled and confused at being awoken so suddenly. Instead of following Adam along the hallway, the little parrot came to find Flora, taking immediate shelter in the folds of her dressing gown. She didn't blame him – Flora herself wanted nothing more than to snuggle down and go to sleep. It had been a long old day.

No such luck, however, since as soon as the front door was opened the vicar let himself in, hurrying into the kitchen. Peeping around the bedroom door, Flora caught her husband's unmistakable expression of 'I'm going to need a hand with this' and so she reluctantly set Reggie down on the bed, closed the door and followed the men into the kitchen.

"Let me get you a drink," Adam said, going straight for the hard stuff in the bottom cupboard.

One look at Cartwright's face and Flora could see exactly why tea wasn't going to cut it. The vicar was a greyish shade of pale, his eyes haunted and his movements jerky, as if he didn't quite have a handle on his body's responses.

"You seem on edge, Christopher," Flora said gently, taking him by the elbow, "why don't we sit in the lounge. It's more comfortable there and you can tell us what's happened. Adam will bring your drink, don't worry." The last she added having seen the man looking longingly at the whisky glass Adam had retrieved from the back of the opposite cabinet.

"Sorry to call so late, I didn't know where else to turn," the vicar said after gulping down the heady spirit in three large mouthfuls. Flora could only imagine the way it must be burning his throat, but the man seemed unbothered.

"Not at all," she replied politely, "I'm guessing it's something urgent?" *Please let's forgo the formalities. My bed's calling!*

"Well, I'd just finished my daily devotions, and had said some rather specific prayers that Genie would get in touch or at least answer my messages, when someone came to the vicarage door. Of course, I hoped God had heard my pleas and sent my beloved to me, but instead it was those two detectives – your friends, Adam," his opinion of the pair in question was clear by the pursing of Cartwright's mouth, as if he'd just tasted something disgusting, and Adam almost felt sullied to be tarred with the same brush as McArthur and Timpson.

Flora could guess what was coming next. No doubt having exhausted their search around the manor house and estate grounds, then around the village, the vicarage would have been the detectives' next port of call in their hunt for Genevieve.

Sure enough, Cartwright continued, "An hour they quizzed me for, as if I was guilty of I-don't-know-what, whilst uniformed officers searched the place from top to bottom. Wouldn't tell me what they were looking for until I put two and two together, realised the questions about the Blanchette sisters and my Genie in particular weren't just general investigations. No! They were trying to find her, my Genevieve! Of course, I asked why, and how long she'd been gone, and how they even knew she was missing and they wouldn't answer me. Wouldn't even give me a definitive yes or no when I asked if she was in danger!" The man was pacing the small sitting room now, making Flora feel rather claustrophobic. She wondered if they should offer him another glass of scotch or if that might make matters worse.

Has he driven here? Flora wondered. His forehead was damp with sweat and his hair slicked back with it, making her think he had run from the vicarage.

"So," Cartwright continued, "the moment they left, I raced up the hill to the big house. I no longer cared if she needed her space, I needed to know if she was okay. They probably followed me, to see if I'd been telling the truth when I told them I knew nothing, but I don't care. There was a guy in uniform stationed at the front door, but I ignored him telling me to go back down. I tried to push past him to hammer on the door, but the young bloke was having none of it. The manor house is in darkness, Flora. There's no one home…"

The man broke down then in silent tears which brought him to his knees.

It was Adam who took a tentative step forward and helped the poor man to the armchair, "Here, mate, have a sit down and I'll tell you what we know. Just between us, alright. You're going to need to be strong, to mentally prepare yourself, because it's going to be a bit of a shock." Flora was moved by her husband's calm composure in preparing the way for the news which was to follow.

"A bit of a shock?" Cartwright parroted back, but the former detective simply nodded, joining Flora on the settee opposite.

"Aye, there's no good way to say this, so I'll just state the facts. A witness has come forward stating they saw a nun disappearing into a secret passageway at The Rise just after the murder was committed. Since Genie was dressed that way and was also the only one who knew of the hidden corridor, she has become the main suspect in the murder investigation. Since this information came to light, Miss Blanchette has been nowhere to be found and so has not had a chance to give her version of events. Hence why the police are very keen to talk with her…"

"…To help them with their enquiries, yes, if I hear that

phrase again this evening I think I'll lose my mind," Cartwright replied, his eyes even wider now if that were possible.

Flora left the two men discussing Genie's possible whereabouts and whether the detectives saw the case as cut and dried whilst she slipped out to put the kettle on. *Chamomile tea all round,* she thought to herself as she tried to comb through her damp hair with her fingers.

"What a sight!" Flora said aloud, catching her reflection in the hallway mirror as she tiptoed around waiting for the water to boil. She paused, a memory trying but failing to come to the surface of her consciousness. When none came, she put the strange, unsettled feeling down to tiredness and returned to the kitchen to make the teas. *All this talk of murder is making me uneasy,* Flora decided, an involuntary shiver running through her despite the mild summer's evening.

"So you don't think Genie's in danger?" The vicar was asking as Flora returned with the tray of drinks.

"I can't be certain of anything," Adam replied with a sad shake of his head, "all we can hope is she comes forward sooner rather than later to say her piece. If the police find her first, it's going to look so much worse."

"If only she'd answer my calls, but her phone just cuts to voicemail now, I think it must be dead," Cartwright said, "and she can't have gone far if she didn't even pack the essentials. I mean, for all we know she could've let herself back into the big house when the majority of the police left and be lying low. She has that big keyring with keys for every door, doesn't she Flora?... Hmm, I think ah, tomorrow morning, yes that's right, tomorrow morning I'll begin my own search."

"I really wouldn't get involved in the police investigation…" Adam began, but the vicar had shot to his feet again, ignoring the cup of tea which Flora was holding out to him.

"I'll be going, thanks for your time," Cartwright said, making a beeline for the door like a man on a mission.

"Well, it's a good job he became a member of the clergy and not an actor," Adam said as they watched the man disappear down the gravel path, "is it just me or did he seem a bit shifty at the end there?"

"Nope, you're spot on, I'd bet my money he's going back up to the manor house, to have a good look inside this time," Flora was already putting on her shoes as

Adam handed her a long raincoat to put on over her pyjamas, having both come to the same conclusion.

If Cartwright was going up to search The Rise, then so were they.

TWENTY-ONE

"Just let him come," Adam said impatiently.

Flora had made the mistake of slipping into the bedroom to get her handbag which had her mobile phone in it, and in doing so she had released the irate parrot who now clutched her shoulder with such force he was probably drawing blood.

"He might be a help," Flora couldn't help but be defensive, after Adam had already questioned why she even needed her bag in the first place. Flora had reminded her husband that he'd previously told her never to go anywhere – let alone investigating – without a means of communication, hence she needed her mobile. In this instance Adam had simply waved his own phone at her, all but stamping his feet in his impatience to get off after the vicar.

"Whatever, let's go," Adam locked the door behind them, as Reggie flew ahead.

"If anyone's in that house and Reggie finds them, he'll certainly let us know," Flora said.

"Yes, just as he'll give anyone the heads up we're coming," Adam countered.

They half-ran, half-walked the rest of the way in sulky silence, neither being as fit as they once were. Reggie, however, was delighted to be free and on an unexpected night-time jaunt, and chattered away to himself happily.

As they approached the uniformed officer at the front door, Adam whispered that he recognised the man and Flora should leave it to him.

"Is that you Detective Bramble, sir?" The man squinted at them, the pale light from the single bulb above the doorway not spreading far enough into the shadows to give clear vision of anyone approaching.

"It is, Chainey, it is. How are you doing, mate? Guessing you drew the short straw, eh?"

"Well, orders is orders, sir, and I've actually just come on duty two minutes ago, took over from young Stafford."

"Let us get you a flask of tea to keep you going then," Bramble said.

"Ah, I've been given my instructions not to let anyone in and to keep an eye out for the suspect, middle-aged woman," the man looked unsure, peering at Flora as if suddenly realising she fit that bill.

Reggie, having had enough of the delay, chose that moment to land on the unsuspecting policeman's head, with a shriek of "Secrets and lies! Hide it all!" that caused the poor bloke to clutch his chest and struggle to catch his breath.

"Reginald Parrot!" Flora chided, "My goodness, I am so sorry. My name is Flora and I own this old house with Adam here. We have the keys to get in, all legal and above board. Please let me calm your nerves with some sweet tea and biscuits."

"You wouldn't even have to leave your post," Adam urged.

"Biscuits you say? Got any custard creams?" The man had made a remarkable recovery from his fright.

"I do, and Bourbon creams," Flora gave her most dazzling smile, all the while tapping the beak of the little bird who was now on her arm, awaiting entrance to his castle.

The Bourbon creams clinched it and Chainey stepped aside with a shrug of the shoulders and a watchful eye on the little parrot, lest he make any more quick moves, "On the down low, eh detective?"

"Absolutely," Adam hurried inside, keen to find the errant clergyman and get back home to his bed.

They switched on lights as they went from the front of the house towards the back, but even so the place felt cold and unlived in. Every creak, every draught had Flora on edge and she almost couldn't believe it had only been a few days since the whole village had been here partying.

"In those scary films, the audience always shouts at the ones who visit the haunted house in the dark with no backup, like they're trying to get themselves killed," Flora tried to make light of her nerves, but only succeeded in making herself feel worse.

"Aye well, thank goodness we're not in a scary film,

eh?" Adam replied, but even he was shining the torch on his phone into every dark corner, poised for action.

Reggie had no such qualms and flew on ahead to the kitchen, no doubt since that was where the fruit was stashed in the big, cold box.

They had just reached the closed door to the kitchen, with Adam telling Flora to stay behind him and let him go in first, when Reggie heard a noise. Immediately, the little bird returned to Flora, snuggling into the crook of her neck and flattening his wings to make himself as small as possible.

"He's frightened," Flora said, the knowledge making the hairs on her own neck stand on end.

They stood silently listening for what had spooked the parrot.

"There," Adam whispered, "Hear that? It's like a scraping sound, wait here."

He inched the door open and entered the large room at the back of the house as stealthily as possible, using the light from the hallway which spilled in behind him and his phone rather than turning on the main lights. The noise seemed to be coming from the back door, and Flora heard Adam mutter a curse and rush over to it.

Unable to help herself, she followed behind and stood by the kitchen table as Adam unlocked the back door from the inside.

"You'd never make a good burglar," he said, rather harshly, at the form of the vicar who was on his knees outside, trying to pick the lock with a paperclip and a bank card.

"I, ah, didn't think this through very well," Cartwright said, blushing, "should've come more prepared."

"Or not come at all," Adam said, the annoyance clear in his tone, "get up and come in, man, we'll do a sweep of the house together while Flora bribes the bobby out front with tea and biscuits. Honestly…" He continued muttering to himself as he led the way, while the vicar gave Flora a sheepish look and scurried after.

"This is the part they find me alone and…" Flora didn't want to finish that thought so instead focused on the task at hand, trying to calm Reggie with some broccoli – the only safe thing for him to eat from the meagre offering in the fridge.

To say the bird was disgusted would be an understatement. The green demon was flung from his mouth in such haste that it hit Flora's cheek, and she quickly removed her naughty pet from her arm.

"Well, it's that or nothing," she said as she went to fill the kettle, "we need to get some more shopping for up here."

"You old trout!" Reggie shrieked, but even he wasn't brave enough to leave the kitchen in his bad temper. The fright from earlier still had him spooked and the little bird stayed close to Flora, who kept her eye on the entrance to the laundry room, half expecting someone to appear from the secret passage down there at any moment.

In the end, there had been nothing so dramatic as a deadly discovery, and sadly nor had they found Genie. The policeman was appeased as promised after the house search, the main doors locked again and the three walked dejectedly back down the gravel driveway with Flora shivering in her night things. Flora and Adam left the vicar to get back to the vicarage with a silent wave as they hurried up the path to the coach house, shutting and locking the door after them. The moment they were inside, Reggie headed straight for the seed tray on his perch in the sitting room as Flora yawned widely and bent to take off her shoes.

"If the woman doesn't turn up soon…" Adam began

ominously, before thinking better of whatever he was about to say and instead finishing with, "Right, bath and bed for me, I think. You go and get cosy, love, I won't be long."

Cosy? Flora thought, *With a friend accused of murder and currently on the run?*

Cosy was the last thing she felt right now.

TWENTY-TWO

Flora tossed and turned all night, dreaming of ghosts walking through walls and of zombies wrapped in Italian flags. As a result, Adam didn't get a good night's sleep either and both were grouchy the next morning. When the alarm went off, Flora hit the snooze button and snuggled back down, safe in the knowledge that Tanya was opening up the tearoom that day. Less than two minutes later, when her mobile phone began to ring loudly, Flora therefore had some choice words to say as she fumbled about on the bedside table to silence the offensive noise.

"Flora? Is that you?" A man's voice asked, though Flora couldn't quite tell who it belonged to since he was talking very fast, "Sorry to bother. Just came into the hallway from the kitchen and seen it on the doormat…"

"Hold on," Flora passed the phone to her husband, as she wiped the sleep from her eyes and tried to think clearly through the grogginess.

"This is Adam Bramble, please start again… Oh, hello Christopher, is everything alright? Has Genie showed up?... What, just now? Did you hear it being posted through? What does it say?... Stay put, we'll be there in twenty."

Flora could only hear her husband's side of the conversation, but even from his expression she could tell it wasn't good news. That and the fact it was seven thirty in the morning – hardly the time for social calls.

"What's happened?" She asked, as she forced herself from the comfort of their bed and began searching in her wardrobe for a sundress.

"He's received another note, much more concerning," Adam replied, pulling on his shirt and already picking up his phone to call McArthur, "I'll get her to meet us at the vicarage, I think we'll need professionals in at the beginning for this one."

Flora finished getting dressed and hurried to the kitchen, a green ball of feathers on her shoulder, tap-tap-tapping with his claws as if to remind her not to leave without getting him his first breakfast of the day. Flora quickly chopped half a banana, eating the remainder herself, and then got two large grapes from the fridge. Seemingly satisfied, Reggie hopped down onto the counter and began stuffing his beak as Flora went through to the sitting room to find her handbag and sandals.

"Let's get going," Adam said impatiently as he finished his call and tied his laces, "Need to act fast on this one."

Flora still had no idea what the message said, but going by the urgency in Adam's tone and actions, time was of the essence.

Driving down Front Street before eight in the morning, Flora would've expected the main road through the village to be quiet. When she spotted a woman walking ahead on the pavement, who from behind looked identical to Betty, she therefore insisted Adam pull over so that Flora could see what had her friend out and about so early. Betty and Harry were not early risers, having a strict routine of tea and toast in bed followed by crochet for her and reading for him. They often didn't bother to get dressed till gone ten. So seeing her friend out in public this early had Flora's anxiety unfurling in her chest.

"We really don't have time, love…" Adam began protesting.

"Now! Stop the car! Just for a second," Flora insisted, jumping out the moment Adam applied the brakes.

"Betty, are you okay?" Flora ran the three steps to her friend and tapped her on the shoulder, shocked when the woman who turned around, looking none too pleased, wasn't in fact Betty at all.

"Oh, I'm sorry! It's that… you look just like…" Flora's voice faded away under the elderly woman's harsh glare.

Flora vaguely recognised her as one of the Women's Institute ladies from Witherham, and felt herself blush hotly at her mistake. Mumbling more apologies she hurried back into the car, to face her husband's exasperated impatience.

"Really, Flora!" Was all he said, but Flora was barely listening. The whirring had started in her head, and she was desperately trying to find what it was prompting her to remember.

Neither spoke again in the couple of minutes it took them to reach the vicarage. Adam parked haphazardly, noting that the detectives hadn't arrived from Morpeth yet – not surprising given that was a journey of about half an hour, and that not accounting for rush hour traffic in the local town. In her haste to exit the vehicle, Flora managed to trap her fingers as she tried to shut the car door. Emitting a loud yelp which caused her husband to come running around to her side, Flora was annoyed to feel tears already leaking from her eyes.

"I'm okay, it just stings," she whispered, lip quivering, giving the digits concerned a tentative wiggle.

"We'll get some ice straight on that, so there's no bruise," Adam said, putting his arm around his wife and hurrying her to the front door of the vicarage.

Flora's mind was whirring uncontrollably now. She knew there were things she should be prompted to recall, and this was distracting her almost as much as the pain in her fingers.

It took a good few moments for the vicar to confirm it was them to his own satisfaction and then to open the heavy wooden door and let them in – by the sounds of it he had the place barricaded up tightly.

"Do you have some ice?" Adam asked the moment they were over the threshold, heading straight for the kitchen at the back.

"Ah, yes? I think there'll be some in the freezer," Cartwright sounded confused by the strange greeting, but followed quickly behind them, clutching an envelope to his chest.

Ice applied, they all sat at the kitchen table, each apparently caught up in their own thoughts.

"So, I take it that's the letter," Adam said, nodding towards the envelope which Cartwright had now placed on the table. The vicar was looking at the missive as if it might jump up and bite him on the nose and used barely the tip of his index finger to push the offensive communication over to Adam.

"Sorry, I forgot to bag it this time," the man said, a quiver to his voice that was not normally there.

"No matter," Adam replied, standing to fetch a piece of kitchen roll which he then used between his fingers and the paper as he removed the single sheet of notepaper from the crumpled envelope, "everything the same as the last two I see."

"Yes, yes, just the message different again," Cartwright said, wringing his hands anxiously. The sight of his white fingers, and the pain in her own, jolted Flora's memory again and she continued to struggle through the brain fog to reach a meaning.

"Hmm," Adam said, his brow furrowed and eyebrows drawn low.

"What does this one say?" Flora asked quietly.

"I may have missed but now you're missing something too," Adam read the single line aloud, causing his wife to gasp.

"And the only one I'm missing is Genie!" The vicar's words came out on a long wail, which Flora felt deep inside herself. That heart-wrenching agony that came from believing you'd lost the one you love.

"Oh my goodness!" Flora's hand flew to her mouth, the whirring calmed and she had total clarity as all of the different pieces of the puzzle clicked into place, "We've been looking at this all wrong! I believe I know where Genie is and who committed the murder!"

TWENTY-THREE

"You've just had an accident love, you're in pain. Christopher, do you have some paraceta…"

"Don't talk down to me, Adam! I don't need to be humoured like the good little woman who's easily confused!" Flora knew the accusation was unfair, but she desperately needed to tell them what she'd remembered.

"Okay," Adam sat back down and Flora had the full attention of both men, "tell us your theory, love."

"Right, ah, where to start. Well, I think this all hinges on the identical fancy dress costumes. The note you've just received, Christopher, says "I may have missed…"

which is exactly what I think happened. I think, unfortunately that you were the murderer's intended target, but given that they had to act quickly, and you were wearing the same clothes…"

"Why would anyone want to kill me?" the vicar asked, shocked.

"Jealousy of your relationship with Genie perhaps? Unable to see her sister so happy? Anyway, ah, back to the beginning. To the murder itself. I was beside the body when Vivienne Blanchette came along the hallway and heard that the doctor had been murdered. I could see Viv's face in the giant ornate mirror that sits on the opposite wall. She was clawing at her chest and screaming 'How could this have happened?' At the time I thought it was agony over her boyfriend's death, now I think it may have been anger and confusion that she had killed the wrong man."

"You mean Viv is the murderer?" Adam asked.

"Quite so," Flora nodded, "but there's more. When I went into the kitchen shortly afterwards and found Genie comforting her sister, Viv's fingers were covered in what I thought at the time were bruises. My own accident just now made me think of them. What if they weren't bruises at all? What if it was the ink residue from the leaking pen used to write the letters the vicar here has received? When we were clearing up after the event, I recall finding similar, unmoveable stains on two white mugs which were only fit for the bin."

Cartwright gasped out loud, "Well, what are we waiting for?"

"Hold on, mate," Adam cautioned, "what about Mrs. May's statement, Flora love?"

"Well, just as I thought that was Betty in the street this morning as she looked identical from behind, what if Hilda May simply saw a nun. Remember, Viv was also dressed in that garb."

"Yes, but as far as we know she didn't know about the secret passage," Adam played Devil's Advocate.

"But what if she did, Adam? Or what if the secret corridor is a red herring and it wasn't used by the murderer at all? What if, Heaven forbid, Viv's angry that her plan went wrong and she's taken it out on Genie? That would account for why she's gone missing…"

"Good Lord!" The vicar shouted, standing suddenly and rushing from the room. Adam and Flora were swift to follow, as the man heaved the heavy vicarage door open to be met with McArthur and Timpson on the doorstep, the latter's hand poised ready to knock.

"Quickly detectives, I'm in need of your vehicle," Cartwright shouted, rushing to the road.

McArthur remained where she was and simply raised an eyebrow at Adam. Understanding the silent question, the former detective gave a single nod and then they were all off, rushing for their cars.

It was a good thing that Adam was paying attention to McArthur's saloon in front as they rushed around the tight country corners, for just as the detective turned into the lane on which the Blanchette house was situated she slammed on the brakes and brought the unmarked police car to a skidding halt. Following suit, Adam also braked sharply, though neither he nor Flora could see what had caused the car in front to stop so suddenly. Reverend Cartwright was the first to jump out of the front vehicle, from the back door, and charged off down the lane. McArthur and Timpson were hot on his heels, so Adam and Flora also left their car in a hurry and followed along behind.

"Genie!" Flora shouted when they all skidded to a halt in front of the couple who were now embracing in the middle of the narrow road. Her own sore fingers forgotten at the sight of her friend.

The vicar had his love in his arms, though from the looks of the poor woman she was decidedly the worse for wear. Her feet were bare and her hair wild.

"Where is your sister?" McArthur asked in a clipped tone, unmoved by the emotional reunion.

"Back in the house, in the hallway," Genie could barely talk through the gasping sobs that wracked her thin frame, "I knocked her out… with a pan… when she got home from delivering the letter… She's still breathing though, I checked."

"We're going to need to hear the full story," McArthur said, dispatching Timpson to restrain the other sister and then radioing for backup and an ambulance.

"Not right now though," Cartwright said, his protective tone brooking no argument, "right now we're getting this lovely woman back to the manor house where she can have a wash and something to eat, change her clothes and start to feel human again, isn't that right Bramble?"

Adam looked to McArthur who must've given her silent agreement – though whatever gesture she used was familiar only between the two of them – as he said,

"Absolutely, let's get her in my car and we'll head up there now."

In the end, Genie's legs were so wobbly that Cartwright lifted her into his arms and carried her to Adam's car, where he lowered her gently onto the back seat, covering her with his blazer before getting in beside her. With Adam and Flora sitting up front, Adam reversed the car back down the lane until it was wide enough to do a U-turn and then made haste for The Rise.

TWENTY-FOUR

"Oh my goodness, no! So you were there listening when we came to Viv's looking for you?" Flora asked, horrified.

"Yes, and when the police came to search the place too. There's a tiny dormer window in the roof at the front of the house that never shuts properly and leaks when it rains so I could hear any visitors arriving. Viv had me tied to one of the beams in the attic at first. That room's only accessible through a narrow, short door on the upstairs landing though, which is covered by the same wood panelling as the wall and which hides a steep staircase behind, so the police mustn't have noticed. Either that, or Viv deliberately blocked it with her body when they were looking around."

"So how did you manage to escape then?" Adam asked, not sounding completely convinced.

"Well, of course she couldn't keep me up there indefinitely as I needed the bathroom and such. My sister isn't a monster. She locked me in my old bedroom when she thought the coast was clear of any more search parties, without realising I learnt to pick that lock as a girl – one too many times being shut in there by my parents. Anyway, I waited until I heard her leaving the house, which I knew she would do soon as she'd bragged about the threatening notes she'd sent to my Christopher here and how she had another one ready. She was so angry, you see. Growing up, it was whenever I had something she didn't, I'd hoped she'd grown out of it…" Genie paused to take a sip of her sweet tea. The colour was returning to her cheeks after the deep bubble bath which Flora had prepared for her, and the fresh clothes warmed on the radiators. "I couldn't get out of the house though, I was trapped with no keys you see, so I waited hidden behind the front door for her to return, then I knocked her out with a pan and ran for my life. Thank goodness you were all there!"

"But why did you even go over there in the first place?" Adam asked, "If you knew she was jealous of you?"

"I'd like to say it was to offer comfort in her grief," a flash of guilt crossed Genie's face, "but really it was to ask her if she'd told anyone about the secret corridor. She saw me using it the other day, you see, when she popped over before the Italian evening and I was decorating the function room. She appeared suddenly, let herself in the back door, and the bookcase door was open when she came into the room so I didn't have a chance to close it before she saw."

"You lied to the police," Adam said, "You told them no one else knew about the passage. If you'd been honest, they'd likely have found you a lot quicker. The detectives aren't stupid, they knew there were two nuns there that evening, but they disregarded Vivienne as a suspect after Mrs. May's statement because you'd told them no one but you knew about the hidden door in the wall. So, they reasoned you were the only nun who would've been disappearing into walls."

"Now hold on, let's not be victim blaming," Cartwright spoke up angrily. He had barely managed to hold his emotions in check through the whole sorry explanation of events.

"No, it's okay Christopher… I know, Adam, and I regretted it straight away. I couldn't let myself believe Viv would've used the passage because that would've made her a murderer and why would she kill her own boyfriend? So, I went round to ask if she'd told anyone else. She welcomed me in, made me a cup of tea and must've drugged me with sedatives or something, because the next I know I'm in the attic."

"But she didn't want to kill her own boyfriend, Doctor Langley, did she?" Flora asked gently.

"No, that's the thing," Genie, who had been remarkably stoic since returning to the big house, broke down now, "she told me that it should've been my Christopher lying dead. That it should've been me grieving and that since it wasn't, one way or another, she was going to hurt me…"

Cartwright pulled the distraught woman onto his lap, where she snuggled into him, as if they were the only two in the whole world.

"She didn't even like Langley," Genie whispered, "couldn't stand the man, but hated the fact I had someone and she didn't even more, so she used him. Just like she uses everyone. She told me that she deliberately chose the same costume as me for the Italian evening so that she could frame me for the murder, could tell everyone I wasn't right in the head and had flown off the handle after a lover's squabble with Christopher here… She was horrid to mother after father died... and then to me, but she was all I had left..." Genie hid her face against Cartwright's chest.

"Let's ah, give you two a moment," Adam said, "no leaving the building though, McArthur will be here shortly."

He and Flora moved to the study, both with solemn expressions and feeling not a small amount of guilt that they hadn't pushed harder when they went to the Blanchette house in search of Genie.

"We weren't to know, love," Adam said, reading Flora's mind and gently pulling her to him for a hug.

"I know, but... it's just all so awful," Flora tried to blink away her own tears, "a man killed in error, and only because of sibling jealousy, an innocent woman held captive and her reputation ruined as everyone labels her a killer... it's just too much for a small village like this! It's almost incomprehensible."

"Well, when you've dealt with this kind of thing as long as I have, this is one of the straightforward ones, believe me," Adam said, wiping Flora's tears with the pad of his thumb, "and you wouldn't believe how many killers are motivated by base human emotions such as jealousy, greed, desire... it's a long list."

"I'm so glad you don't work in that field any longer," Flora said, "I imagine you can't help but be tainted by it."

"Well, I've shoved it all in a metaphorical box, love, and I don't intend to open it anytime soon."

Flora understood all too well, as she had one of those boxes in her own head – one that was getting fuller the longer she lived in Baker's Rise.

TWENTY-FIVE

Two weeks had passed since Genie was found and her sister arrested. Vivienne had been taken to the hospital in Morpeth and treated for a concussion before being transferred to the police station for questioning. According to McArthur, she had admitted everything, actually been proud of it, well, other than the fact she had killed the wrong man. That rather large detail apparently ate away at the woman, who was still keen to correct her mistake and talked at length about how she would make her sister and the vicar pay. Thankfully, the murderer was now safely behind bars and everyone was safe from her toxic jealousy.

Genie too, had been checked over by a doctor in Alnwick the day she was found and given the all-clear, provided she rest for a few days and consider some talking therapy for her trauma – both recent and historical. She had considerable bruising where she appeared to have been dragged up into the attic room, and that was nothing compared to how much her heart hurt at her sibling's betrayal. Christopher Cartwright barely left her side other than to sleep at the vicarage and speak in church on Sundays, and Flora had deliberately avoided the big house to give the couple some space to recover in private.

Edwards had suggested he re-take the reins and become the village's interim doctor, to which the response from the parish council was a resounding no.

"No doctor is better than that doctor," Harry Bentley proposed, and all assembled agreed.

This left the small matter of filling the role, though, and that process was still ongoing.

As was her way after these decidedly unsettling events, Flora threw herself into her comforting daily routine at the tearoom and bookshop. Adam, too, seemed more than happy to lay down his detective's mantle for good and was considering writing a memoir of his experiences or perhaps a fictional thriller drawing on his professional knowledge. They rubbed along nicely, with nothing on the horizon to shake the calm current of village life.

Which was why Flora was worried that Friday morning when her husband appeared from the bookshop with a strange look on his face. Flora couldn't quite place it, it was part fear, part excitement – certainly, he looked like he was bursting to share whatever news he had received.

"Can I have a word, love?" He asked, raising a few eyebrows amongst the women whose table Flora was currently clearing.

"Good news, is it?" Betty asked.

"She's a corker!" Reggie exclaimed, helping himself to the remains of the older woman's scone while her attention was momentarily diverted.

"You'll find out in good time," Adam replied, putting his arm around his wife's waist and hurrying her through to the bookish side of the old building, not even bothering to give the parrot a small lecture on hygiene as he normally would.

"That was a bit rude," Flora let out a small, nervous giggle.

"Aye well, so's her being nosy! Can't a couple have a bit of privacy?"

"Well, there's no one else in here, so what is it? Something about the case?"

"What? No, no, I've told McArthur I don't need any more updates. Genie is healing and safe, her sister is in custody, I don't need to know any more than that. No, the phone call I just received was from a different department altogether."

Flora felt her heartrate increase and prayed she could predict what he was about to say next. Last week, one of the fostering team from Northumberland council had come to do another house check at the manor and they were waiting to hear if it had all been signed off as safe again, "Is it about the house? Are we back on the good-to-go emergency fostering list?"

"More than that love," Adam could barely keep still now, so great was his nervous agitation, "she said they have a placement for us! Someone who needs a longer-term home at that! I told her I'd have to speak with you, of course, but if you agree then by tonight we'll be foster parents!"

Flora sank down onto the squishy beanbag in the corner in shock. It was what she wanted, with her whole heart it was, but now that the dream had become a reality she felt quite overwhelmed.

"Well, the room's ready with cuddly toys and books. The bed is made up with Winnie the Pooh covers. Oh! Should I buy some nappies? Did she say what size?"

"Actually love, if you'd let me finish, there's more to tell you. You see, it's not a toddler or even a child at primary school. Her name's Naomi and she's just turned thirteen."

"Thirteen?" Flora squawked, in a good impersonation of Reggie.

"Aye love, that's okay, isn't it? We did put ourselves down for any age."

"We did, I know, it's just… a small shock. Nothing to worry about. All in hand," Flora raised her arm so that her husband could hoist her indelicately from the ridiculously low and squashy piece of furniture and began making a list out loud, "I'll make up a welcome basket, like a self-care kit, we don't know what she'll have with her, with deodorant, a notebook, some of those gel pens the girls like from Jean's… and some of those cashmere bed socks that Rosa knits for her shop, and some banana loaf from Lily's farm shop. Or do you think chocolate loaf? Teenage girls love chocolate, don't they?"

"Breathe love, just breathe, I'll phone back and say we're happy then we can take a walk into the village and get all the bits you've mentioned. I'll ask Tanya to stay on here an extra hour or two and we'll get it all sorted. No panic, no stress, okay?" His words were sensible and would've been calming had Adam's brow not erupted in droplets of sweat and the muscle beside his eye begun to bounce in nervous agitation.

"Yes, it'll all be fine," Flora rubbed her husband's arm soothingly and tried to control her own breathing.

Foster parents to a teenager? This may well be our biggest challenge yet!

TWENTY-SIX

Genie and Reverend Cartwright had thoughtfully gone out to give them some space and privacy, whilst Flora had had a whip round the place, polishing and hoovering like a mad woman, despite the fact the housekeeper herself was well on top of things. The bed covers in the girl's bedroom had been changed to a much more floral design, and some more age-appropriate books added from the bookshop. Flora laid out the welcome basket on top of the white chest of drawers and lamented that she hadn't had time to get a desk.

"It's perfect," Adam said, joining her with a bucket and mop in his hand, having just finished cleaning the main bathroom as instructed. It was an old house, so no en-suites and Flora hoped their new arrival wouldn't mind.

"Well, it's as good as I can make it at short notice," Flora said, removing her apron and following her husband out of the room.

"It's perfect, love, believe me and I know, it'll be a palace compared to what she's used to."

Reggie had been quite bemused by the whole thing. At first, sensing Flora's nervous excitement, he had followed her around, hoping the source of the energy in the air would be revealed, and preferably be of the edible variety. When, however, he realised that housework and cleaning were all that was on the menu he made a swift exit for his perch in the study, where he now sat snoring. That was until the heavy clap of the front door knocker roused him suddenly, and he flew into the hallway and onto Flora's shoulder.

"No, Reggie, perch please," Flora tried to shoo the inquisitive bird back, but he was having none of it and there wasn't time to physically return him to the room as Adam was already opening the door to their guests. "Best behaviour," Flora warned.

Of course, the social work team already knew about

the parrot, and he had been included in their risk assessment, but the teenager's eyes bulged wide when she saw the bird. Still, she didn't say a word, not even when prompted to introduce herself by the kind lady dropping her off. Flora more than made up for the silence, however, filling it with her own nervous chatter. The social worker didn't have time for the tea and cake which Flora had prepared, and before she knew it they had said goodbye to the professional and were left sitting awkwardly on the velvet settees in the drawing room.

Again, to fill the silence, Flora quickly told Naomi about her bedroom and the gardens.

"Perhaps it'll be easier to take her on a tour love, and let her settle in at her own pace," Adam suggested, "would that be okay, Naomi?"

Instead of answering the question she'd been asked, the newcomer turned her gaze back to Reggie, on whom she had been transfixed for most of the time, and said, "Does it bite?"

"Who Reggie? Oh, only murderers! Haha!" Flora was horrified, but the words were out before she could stop them.

Adam let out a strange cough that sounded almost like

choking and his eyebrows flew into his hairline.

The girl's eyes widened, but thankfully she moved the conversation along without pause, "Can I hold him?"

"Well, Reggie chooses who he goes to, and since he's been so well behaved since you've been here, I fear we may be due for an outburst," Flora replied gently, "but some grapes normally do the trick to make him like you. Would you like to get him some from the fridge? We could go into the kitchen?"

Naomi nodded, and Flora let out a sigh of relief that they'd broken the ice.

Perhaps Reggie would be her secret weapon in bonding with her new foster daughter – who would've thought it!

"Nay-oh-mee" Flora was sitting at the kitchen table with Reggie and Naomi later that evening, having had a big meal of spaghetti bolognese, and they were now trying to teach the parrot his new friend's name.

"No Me! No Me!" Reggie squawked, being deliberately difficult Flora knew – after all, he had picked up much more complicated words than this. Whole sentences in fact.

"No me neither!" Naomi giggled, and it touched Flora's heart to hear the girl laugh for the first time. She had come with a small rucksack of all her worldly belongings, and in the tiny moments she and Adam had had to talk alone since the teenager's arrival, Flora had told her husband that she intended to do everything she could to improve Naomi's life while she was with them.

As bedtime approached, Naomi fell silent once more, and couldn't even be roused by a cup of hot chocolate with cream. Flora was unsure what to do, but it was getting late and she and Adam had had an exhausting day. They had brought up enough clothes for the next week from the coach house before cleaning the whole place – they would get the rest of their things over the weekend – and Flora ached all over. That being said, she didn't want to dispatch her new charge off to bed if the girl was feeling upset or uncomfortable.

Not sure how best to broach the subject, Flora needn't have worried as Reggie hopped from the table to Naomi's shoulder, earning him a smile from his new friend.

"So cosy! No Me!" Reggie squawked, and was rewarded with a tickle under the chin from the girl.

"Can um, I mean, I'm not so good with the dark. Can

Reggie stay in my room?" Naomi whispered, avoiding all eye contact with Flora and keeping her focus firmly on the parrot.

Flora wondered why she herself hadn't thought of that.

"What a grand idea," Adam said, coming in from the hallway where he had been locking the front of the house up. Genie was already in her bedroom, having said a brief hello when she returned from the vicarage. "I'll take his perch from the study up. Sometimes he likes to sleep in his cage at the end of the upstairs hallway, but if you leave your bedroom door open slightly and I leave the landing light on, then he can go there if he wants without disturbing you."

And so her husband managed to reassure their daughter that there would be a light on, without adding to her discomfort or embarrassment, and Flora wasn't sure she'd ever loved him more than in that moment.

"Mamma mia! She's a corker!" Reggie squealed in excitement when he realised he was actually being allowed to sleep in a bedroom, and with a person there too – something he was used to doing at the coach house but had been prohibited from doing in the big house until now.

The perch was repositioned into Naomi's room and Flora said a quick goodnight, leaving the girl and the bird to it. She had already shown Naomi where the bathroom and essentials were earlier in the day, and felt that it must've been overwhelming enough for the girl. Any more explanations and directions could surely wait till the morning.

"She's a keeper!" Flora heard Reggie squawk as she paused outside the room.

"I hope so, Reggie," Naomi replied, "I never get to stay anywhere for long before they want me gone."

"My No Me!" Reggie replied, and Flora hurried to her own room two doors down with a lump in her throat the size of Everest, knowing she would do everything in her power to give this girl the security and home she deserved.

TWENTY-SEVEN

Since it was Saturday the next day, Naomi accompanied Flora and Reggie to the tearoom whilst Adam made a trip to Ikea to get a desk and chair for the teenager's room. They had offered to move the cuddly toys out, but the girl had looked at them with a certain longing in her eye and said no, they could stay. After a good night's sleep, Naomi looked less gaunt and the rabbit-caught-in-the-headlights look was fading from her eyes – something Flora knew she had Reggie to thank for.

The little parrot had eaten a gargantuan breakfast of fruit salad, hand fed to him by Naomi and no doubt confirming in the little bird's head that he really was the royalty he believed himself to be. A new bedroom and a new person at his beck and call? Reggie felt like Christmas and a lottery win must've come at once!

Flora had only had time to show Naomi around the bookshop and tearoom before their first customers arrived – none other than Betty and Hilda May, the latter having returned to her mouselike shyness since her performance at the Italian evening.

Poor woman, she lets her hair down for once, only to be questioned by the police and scared half to death by an apparent ghost! Flora didn't think she'd be repeating it any time soon.

"Ooh and who do we have here then?" Betty asked, smiling at Naomi.

Protective of his new friend, Reggie flew from his perch onto Naomi's shoulder and replied, "No Me! My No Me!" which made the girl in question blush happily.

"This is Naomi," Flora explained, "she'll be staying with us for a while." She had already told her friends of the plan to foster, so Betty immediately understood.

"Well, you've landed on your feet here in Baker's

Rise," Betty declared, patting the seat next to her for Naomi to sit down, "best village in England, and we look after our own. You're one of us now!"

"Welcome to the tearoom!" Reggie added from Naomi's shoulder, as if confirming she was in the right place, and with a warning look to little Tina the terrier on Betty's knee as if to say, 'she's mine!'

The teenager sat down with only a small moment of hesitation as Flora went to make a pot of Earl Grey, keeping an ear on the conversation, as Betty was not known for her tact.

"Can you knit, lass?" Betty asked, to a shake of the head from Naomi, who stroked Reggie's feathers continuously as if for comfort. Of course, the little parrot himself wasn't complaining! "Well, we'll get you sorted with your first set of knitting needles, very special that is, and some yarn from Rosa's. And how about baking?"

"Ah, no, just some fairy cakes in school," Naomi whispered.

"Then you'll get to learn from a master!" Betty nodded so strongly that her curls bounced wildly under her straw summer hat.

The teenager looked around the room, as if expecting to see a person in a chef's hat appear, before she clocked on that Betty was referring to herself, "Ah, thank you, Mrs…um.."

"You can call me Granny Betty, lass, we're going to have a lot of fun together."

And once again Flora's heart did a small leap of joy and she felt like kissing her friend for her generous nature and kind-hearted welcome – much the same as the welcome she herself had received a couple of years ago.

"Did you hear about the Marshalls?" Betty asked, around a mouthful of lemon drizzle cake.

"No?" Flora, who had come to sit at the table as there were no other customers had the sudden worry that Sally may have had a relapse, "Nothing bad, I hope?"

"What? Oh no, I heard from Mrs. Birch, who heard from her sister who knows the family they're staying with down south, that the Marshall family are coming back home to Baker's Rise next Saturday! Of course, as soon as I heard I rushed round to the vicarage and strongly suggested to Reverend Cartwright that he might want to put on a special welcome home for them. I mean, I know the man's all loved up with your housekeeper, but standards mustn't be let slip, eh? This is Baker's Rise and not Witherham after all."

Flora could well imagine how that conversation had gone, and shared a wry smile with Naomi, who seemed to be enjoying Betty's forthright personality greatly.

"I'll speak with him after the church service tomorrow and see what we can arrange," Flora said, "I assume the W.I. would be happy to cater the event?"

"Of course," Betty replied brusquely, as if it went without saying, "especially since we have our new helper here." She linked her arm through Naomi's and gave the girl another slice of lemon cake from the plate in the middle of the table. Hilda May poured the rest of the lemonade from the glass bottle into Naomi's glass and the girl blushed under the attention of not one, but two new grandmas.

Baker's Rise might actually be the best village in England, Flora thought happily, *if you disregard the murder statistics and focus on the good people...*

TWENTY-EIGHT

The week had gone remarkably smoothly, with Naomi catching the school bus that went through the village up to her high school in Alnwick. She was happy that she didn't have to leave her friends, and had even chatted a bit about them to Flora in the evenings. The village was buzzing with the plans to welcome the Marshall family back to Baker's Rise with a garden party on the vicarage lawn that Saturday, and everyone had been roped into providing something, be it decorations, tableware, food or music.

The day of the garden party dawned clear and warm, with not a cloud in the sky. Flora and Naomi had enjoyed a shopping trip the evening before in Alnwick after school, and had both chosen a new summer dress for the occasion as well as having their hair done and their nails painted. Flora couldn't explain the joy it gave her to share these things with her foster daughter, and Naomi too had been glowing with all the attention. Jean had dropped off a tiny, felt bow tie which she'd made for Reggie especially for the occasion, and he strutted around the kitchen table at The Rise as Genie helped Flora gather up the trays of cannoli they had made for the party. For once, Flora had found a sweet treat she was actually good at making and enjoyed doing, and since the Marshall family had missed the Italian evening – probably for the best by all accounts – Flora thought she could share a taste of it with them now.

The whole village and most of Witherham too had congregated on the lawn at the vicarage. Luckily, the family had arrived back the previous evening and had had some time to get unpacked and get some sleep before being inundated with well-wishers.

"You're new," Flora heard little Evie Marshall say to Naomi, and was about to answer for her daughter – since the whole event was probably overwhelming enough without being interrogated – when Naomi responded gently, "I am, I'm Naomi, what's your name?"

"No Me! No Me!" Reggie chanted from the teenager's shoulder, as Evie introduced herself and the girls got chatting. Despite the age difference, they had a common friend in Reggie and so had plenty of his antics to share. Even quiet Charlotte was giggling at the stories, as little Megan clung to Sally's leg and tried to shove a whole cupcake into her mouth in one go.

"You really shouldn't have," Sally said to Flora, looking better than she had even before her diagnosis.

"Well, it's a pleasure, but let's just say no one would've been allowed to not take part…" Flora raised an eyebrow in Betty's direction and Sally smiled.

"I see nothing has changed in Baker's Rise then," the vicar's wife said.

"Only with regards to the Blanchette sisters," Flora whispered, to which Sally nodded wordlessly. Thankfully, Reverend Cartwright had already updated them on that sad story.

They were then interrupted by the clanking of metal on glass as Cartwright himself tried to get the group's attention – by no means an easy feat. When, at last, the crowd fell silent, he made a toast to the returning family, expressed his relief that he no longer had to shoulder serving the tri-parish community himself, and then asked if everyone would allow him to ask a personal question.

This caused the ears of all assembled to perk up in renewed interest, as the man got down on one knee and began laying his heart bare to Genie Blanchette, who had tears streaming down her face.

"I bet they'll be married before I can say wedding cake," Betty said in a stage whisper to Jean who nodded happily.

When the appropriate toasts had been made to the newly engaged couple, and Genie had been given every opportunity to show off her beautiful ring, Adam and Flora took the happy couple off to one side. They had had some searching conversations between themselves and had come to a decision which they hoped Genie and the vicar would be happy with.

"As you know," Adam said when it was just the four of them, "we have Naomi now and so are living up at the manor house. Since we're hoping she'll be a long-term addition to our family, Flora and I have made the decision to move out of the coach house. Now, as you're to be wed, and the vicarage is pretty full again and you might like some privacy, we wondered how you'd feel about living in the coach house?"

"Oh my goodness," Genie was visibly shocked, "Are you sure, Flora? I know how much you've enjoyed living there."

"I am," Flora felt the bittersweet moment deep in her chest – the happiness of a fresh start and family life in the big house, tempered with the sadness of moving out of the cosiest, homeliest home she had ever had, "I'm ready to make the move permanent."

"Wow, this was already the happiest day of my life, and now you've solved the only problem I had weighing me down," Cartwright said, his eyes shiny, "my affianced here has already decided she doesn't want to move into her family home – too many bad memories, eh love."

"Sadly, yes, I'll have it put on the market by the end of the summer. But no talk of unhappy things now. Not today. Though, I'm not sure I can take any more wonderful surprises in one day," Genie said, hugging her fiancé as she shed more tears of pure joy.

Flora and Adam moved away to give the couple some privacy and shared their own happy moment with Naomi and Reggie who had come to find them. They were a foursome now, an unlikely quartet maybe, but one formed through love and connection.

Flora couldn't be happier with her little family.

Will the pattern of home-spun life stay as simple when the infamous 'Yarn Wars' comes to film in the village, or will the façade of friendly rivalry slip somewhat?

*Find out in **"A Stitch in Key Lime,"** the tenth book in the **Baker's Rise Mysteries** series.*

A cosy new series is out now featuring Reverend Daisy Bloom and her rather secretive neighbours.

"Fresh as a Daisy," *the first instalment in the **Lillymouth Mysteries** series set in North Yorkshire.*

Read on for an excerpt…

AN EXCERPT FROM *FRESH AS A DAISY* – *THE LILLYMOUTH MYSTERIES BOOK ONE*

Daisy Bloom hummed along to the Abba song on Smooth radio, pondering how she might use the lyric 'knowing me, knowing you' this coming Sunday, in the first sermon she would deliver in her new parish. She was barely concentrating on her driving in fact, knowing the roads like the back of her hand as she did. Barely anything changed around here, in this small coastal corner of Yorkshire, and Daisy really wasn't sure if that was a good thing or not. It had been fifteen years since she had left the town of Lillymouth, at the tender age of eighteen, and the newly ordained vicar had not been back since. Indeed, had the Bishop himself not personally decreed this was the parish for her – in some misguided attempt to help her chase away the demons of her past, Daisy presumed – then she suspected that she would not have come back now either.

Positives, think about the positives, Daisy told herself, pushing a finger between her dog collar and her neck to let a bit of air in. The weather was remarkably lovely for early July in the North of England, and Daisy was regretting wearing the item which designated her as a member of the clergy. She had wanted to arrive at her new vicarage with no possibility that they not immediately recognise her as the new incumbent – after that awful time when she turned up as the curate of her last parish, and they had mistaken her as the new church organist. Not helped by the fact that she was tone deaf… She knew she looked very different from the fresh-faced girl who had left town under a black cloud though, so there was a good chance even the older townsfolk wouldn't recognise her.

Anyway, positive thoughts, positive thoughts, Daisy allowed her mind to wander to the shining light, the beacon of hope for her return to this little town – her new goddaughter and namesake, Daisy Mae, daughter of her best friend from high school, Bea. Pulling up outside of the bookshop which her friend owned, and glad to have found a disabled parking spot so close, Daisy was surprised to find she was relieved that the old Victorian building had not changed since she left all those years ago. It still stood tall and proud on the bottom corner of Cobble Wynd and Front Street, it's wooden façade hinting at its age. The building had been a bookshop since Edwardian times, Daisy knew, and she smiled as she saw the window display was filled with baby books and toys – old and new coming together in harmony, something that, according to the Bishop, was far from happening in the town as a whole.

"Daisy!" the familiar voice brought a sudden lump to her throat as Daisy made her way into the relative dimness of the shop, the smell of books and coffee a welcome comfort. The voice of the woman who had been her childhood friend, who had been one of the few to support her when the worst happened all those years ago... *positive thoughts...*

"Bea," Daisy leant her walking stick against the old wooden counter and reached out to hug her friend, careful that her own ample bosom didn't squash the little baby that was held in a carrier at her mother's chest. Wanting to say more, but finding herself unable to speak around her emotion, Daisy tried to put all of the love and affection she could into that physical touch.

"Meet Daisy Mae," Bea said proudly, pulling back and

turning sideways so that Daisy could see the baby's face.

"The photos didn't do her justice, Bea, really, she's beautiful." Okay, now the feelings had gone to her eyes, and Daisy tried to wipe them discreetly with the back of her hand. She wasn't this person, who was so easily moved – or at least she hadn't been since she ran and left Lillymouth behind. Daisy had funded herself through training and then worked as a police support officer for victims of violence for almost a decade, before hearing the calling to serve a higher purpose. She had survived assault and injury as part of her previous profession, seen some truly horrible things, and yet had not felt as emotional as she did now. Not since the day she quit this place, in fact…

"Aw, you must be tired from the drive," Bea, tactful and sensitive as always, gave her the perfect 'out', "come and have a cuppa and a sandwich in the tea nook. Andrew just finished refurbishing it for me."

"Thank you, but let me get it for you, are you even meant to be working so soon after the birth?"

"I'm just covering lunchtimes while my maternity cover nips out for a quick bite – well, I think she's actually meeting her boyfriend, she never manages to stick to just the one hour, but, ah, she's young and well read… why don't you hold little Daisy while I get us sorted with something?"

"Oh! I… well, I…"

"You'll be fine, Daisy, you're going to have a lot of babies to hold during christenings, you know! I can't wait for you to christen this little one," Bea chuckled and unfastened the baby pouch, handing the now squirming bundle to the vicar without hesitation once Daisy had lowered herself into a squashy leather armchair.

Wide, deep blue eyes, the colour of the swell in Lillywater Bay on a stormy day looked up at Daisy with surprise and she found herself saying a quick prayer that the baby wouldn't start to scream. Daisy desperately wanted to be a part of this little girl's life, feeling as she did that she might never have a child of her own. What she had seen in her previous profession had put Daisy off relationships for life. As part of the Church of England she was not forbidden from getting married and starting a family – quite the opposite – but Daisy's own feelings on the matter ran deep and dark.

"Here we go," Bea returned with a tray holding a pot of tea, two china mugs, a plate of sandwiches and some cakes, "you look like you could do with this."

"You aren't wrong there," Daisy felt suddenly and surprisingly bereft as baby Daisy Mae was lifted gently from her arms and placed in a pram in the corner next to them.

"Have you visited the vicarage yet? Nora will be on tenterhooks waiting for you, she'll have Arthur fixing and cleaning everything, poor man!"

"I haven't had that pleasure," Daisy smiled ruefully, "I thought I'd come to visit my two favourites first," Daisy smiled back, knowing she was being slightly cowardly, but Nora Clumping was not a woman to become reacquainted with on an empty stomach. She had been the housekeeper at the vicarage for as long as Daisy could remember, surviving numerous clergy, and she had seemed ancient to Daisy as a girl. She could only imagine how old the woman must be now. She must have a soft side though, Daisy had thought to herself on the journey from Leeds, otherwise she wouldn't have taken Arthur in decades ago and adopted him as her own. Not that that diminished from the woman's formidable presence, however… for someone so slight in stature, she was certainly a powerhouse to contend with!

"Ah, wise choice," Bea agreed, "and if I were you, I'd

pick up some fruit scones from Barnes the Baker's before you head up there!"

"Sound advice," Daisy laughed out loud, before remembering the baby who had now fallen back asleep, and lowered her voice to a whisper to joke, "I may be in the church now, but I'm not above the odd bit of bribery where necessary!"

"Just wait till you hear her views on the previous vicar," Bea said, not a small amount of excitement in her voice, "oh how I wish I could be a fly on the wall!"

"Argh," Daisy groaned exaggeratedly into her coffee mug causing her friend to snort.

"I want all the details afterwards," Bea continued, "I'll bet you five pounds that within ten minutes she mentions that time she caught you making a daisy chain with flowers you'd pulled from the vicarage garden."

"I was eight!" Daisy replied in mock protest, even while still knowing her friend was right – nothing was ever forgotten in small towns like these.

"Well, I've still got your back like I did then," Bea said, reaching over to rub Daisy's shoulder conspiratorially, and adding with a wink, "and I'm sure she isn't allowed to give the new vicar chores as punishment!"

Perhaps coming back to this place after so long won't be so bad after all, Daisy thought. *With good friends like this, I can serve the parish, find the justice I seek for Gran and be out of here before the Bishop can say 'Amen.'*

The Bible says 'seek ye first the Kingdom of God' – well, I've done that, now I can seek out a cold hearted killer. They may have gotten away with it for over a decade, but divine retribution is about to be served.

A Stitch In Key Lime

Baker's Rise Mysteries Book Ten

Publication Date: 7th November 2023

Join Flora, Reggie and the residents of Baker's Rise in this tenth instalment of the popular series, where it's a case of knitting needles at dawn in the biggest crafting competition the village has seen!

Excitement abounds amongst the ladies of Baker's Rise as a TV crew arrive to film an episode of the popular "Yarn Wars" show. The usually tight-knit bunch are quickly at odds, however, in their quest to be crowned the contest queen and life on set is far from being a ball.

Unfortunately, it's a case of knit one, purl one, kill one as somebody doesn't seem to be following the proper pattern. Certainly, the discovery of a dead body is enough for more than one contestant to drop a stitch and for the whole production to unravel.

Will Flora be able to thread the loose ends together before one of the villagers is stitched up for a crime they didn't commit?

Packed with twists and turns, and enough purls of

wisdom to keep you hooked, this new mystery will certainly leave you hungry for more!

Fresh as a Daisy

The Lillymouth Mysteries Book One

Out now!

A new mystery series from R. A. Hutchins, author of the popular Baker's Rise Mysteries, combines the charm of a Yorkshire seaside town with the many secrets held by its inhabitants to produce a delightful, cosy page-turner.

When Reverend Daisy Bloom is appointed to the parish of Lillymouth she is far from happy with the decision. Arriving to find a dead body in the church grounds, leaves her even less so.

Reacquainting herself with the painful memories of her childhood home whilst trying to make a fresh start, Daisy leans on old friends and new companions. Playing the part of amateur sleuth was never in her plan, but needs must if she is to ever focus on her own agenda.

Are her new neighbours all as they seem, or are they harbouring secrets which may be their own undoing? Worse still, will they also lead to Daisy's demise?

A tale of homecoming and homicide, of suspense and secrets, this is the first book in the Lillymouth Mysteries Series.

No Shrinking Violet

The Lillymouth Mysteries Book Two

Publication Date 20th June 2023

With a new, unexpected ally, a housekeeper who enjoys amateur sleuthing and the unwanted affections of an otherwise aloof vicarage cat, Reverend Daisy Bloom is back in this second book of the popular Lillymouth Mysteries series.

Tensions are high in Lillymouth as some of the locals attempt to move a group of environmental activists who have settled on the headland just outside of town. Leading the way is Violet Glendinning, wife of the local bank manager, head of the parish council, and self-appointed protector of 'the way things used to be.'

Daisy is reluctantly given the role of keeper of the peace, though she would much rather be focusing on her own personal conflicts.

When one of the newcomers is found dead shortly after an altercation with Violet, it is not long before she finds herself faced with uncomfortable enquiries.

Will Violet swallow her pride and ask Reverend Daisy for help, or will it prove too bitter a pill to swallow?

ABOUT THE AUTHOR

Rachel Hutchins lives in northeast England with her husband, three children and their dog Boudicca. She loves writing both mysteries and romances, and enjoys reading these genres too! Her favourite place is walking along the local coastline, with a coffee and some cake!

You can connect with Rachel and sign up to her quarterly **newsletter** via her website at: www.authorrachelhutchins.com

Alternatively, she has social media pages on:

Facebook: www.facebook.com/rahutchinsauthor

Instagram: www.instagram.com/ra_hutchins_author

OTHER BOOKS BY R. A. HUTCHINS

The Angel and the Wolf

What do a beautiful recluse, a well-trained husky, and a middle-aged biker have in common?
Find out in this poignant story of love and hope!

When Isaac meets the Angel and her Wolf, he's unsure whether he's in Hell or Heaven.
Worse still, he can't remember taking that final step.
They say that calm follows the storm, but will that be the case for Isaac?

Fate has led him to her door,
Will she have the courage to let him in?

To Catch A Feather
Found in Fife Book One

When tragedy strikes an already vulnerable Kate Winters, she retreats into herself, broken and beaten. Existing rather than living, she makes a journey North to try to find herself, or maybe just looking for some sort of closure.

Cameron McAllister has known his own share of grief and love lost. His son, Josh, is now his only priority. In his forties and running a small coffee shop in a tiny Scottish fishing village, Cal knows he is unlikely to find love again.

When the two meet and sparks fly, can they overcome their past losses and move on towards a shared future, or are the memories which haunt them still too real?

These books, as well as others by Rachel, can be found on Amazon worldwide in e-book and paperback formats, as well as free to read on Kindle Unlimited.

Printed in Great Britain
by Amazon